I

fore the

Valerie Mason-John (aka Queenie) was born in Cambridge in 1962. She has worked as an international correspondent covering a range of stories from Australian Aboriginal Land Rights, to interviewing Sinn Fein prisoners in Maghaberry Prison, Northern Ireland, and contributed to the *Guardian*, *The Voice* and the *Morning Star*. She has written two non-fiction books documenting the lives of African and Asian women in Britain, has written and produced several plays, and has a collection of prose, poetry and plays published. She currently works as a trainer in forum theatre, drama and creative writing for temper control and conflict resolution. Winner of the Windrush Achievement Award: Arts and Community Pioneer 2000, and winner of the inaugural Shorelines Competition for Black British African, Asian and Caribbean writers, she lives in South London. *Borrowed Body* is her first novel.

Borrowed Body

Valerie Mason-John

A complete catalogue record for this book can be obtained
from the British Library on request

The right of Valerie Mason-John to be identified as the author
of this work has been asserted by her in accordance with the
Copyright, Designs and Patents Act 1988

Copyright © 2005 Valerie Mason-John

First published by Serpent's Tail
4 Blackstock Mews, London N4 2BT
Website: www.serpentstail.com

Designed and typeset by Sue Lamble
Printed by Mackays of Chatham, plc

10 9 8 7 6 5 4 3 2 1

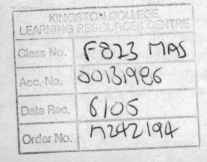

Acknowledgements

My favourite part of the book is the thank you list, because it reminds me that more than one person has helped me bring a book into full bloom. There are my friends, family, and you the readers who have all helped by encouraging me and supporting my work. Thank you. Special thanks to my supervisor Catherine Smith, at Sussex University, where the novel first gave birth. Thank you for wholeheartedly believing in it, and the insightful feedback which carried me to the end. Thank you to Peter Kalu and Tariq Mehmood for having the idea to launch a competition for black writers; it was that which gave me the inspiration to write. To my blood sister, Suna Simbo Smythe, for supporting me and encouraging me to write this novel. To Carol Gallaghar, Nigel Thompson, Shirley McKoy, Sharon Dolphin, Jacky Nelson for their memories and anecdotes of life in the '70s and '80s. To Valerie Witonska, Francis Connelly, Eva Lewin, Jackie Clarke and Muditasari for reading early drafts and giving me constructive feedback. Thank you to Obufemi Adewumi for taking care of my computer, Charles Banjoko for help with the pidgin English and Errol John for his continued support. Finally many thanks to my publisher Pete Ayrton, editor Ruthie Petrie and the rest of the Serpents Tail team, for believing in the novel. Thank you.

Pauline

1

I could have been born and raised in Africa. But my Spirit
was in too much of a rush to be reincarnated. Instead I
borrowed the body of a Nigerian woman who was trying to
escape her life by setting sail to the land of Milk and Honey. I
thought I saw two lovers lying together on the flower-strewn
banks of the river Oshun. So I said to myself here's the
chance I've been waiting for. I jumped inside her body in the
hopes that this time round I would be a love child.

Last time I was aborted at three months, pierced through
the uterus by a knitting needle. I was the eleventh child. My
brothers and sisters before me had exhausted all my parents'
energy and resources. And so I vowed that now I would be
the firstborn, conceived out of love.

Unknown to me, this woman had given birth before. She
had dumped a four-year-old girl onto her relatives on the
outskirts of Lagos. Arriving pregnant in England was most
definitely not part of this Nigerian woman's plan. So I
played dead in her stomach to avoid an abortion. Until one
day a doctor said: "Sorry, Miss Charles, it's not fibroid cysts
after all. It's a twenty-week-old healthy baby snuggled up
inside your womb."

I could tell from her heartbeat that she resented the fact I had chosen her. Her blood, red with fury, whipped its way through the umbilical cord as if to flog me to death. I realised then I had made a blunder. It was not love, but hate, which was bringing me into the world; she had been a victim of rape.

So my impatience got me into trouble, and I've been paying for it ever since. But I had been roaming the ether for hundreds of years, and I thought it was about time I was reborn. The year was 1965.

I was cut out before my time, five weeks too early, just before the festive season. Then at six weeks I was chucked out into the new year, abandoned on a harsh English winter's day which wasn't prepared to welcome an African baby.

White healthy babies were still in demand and so a white family had to be tempted by money to foster me. Ten months later they realised there were easier ways of raising cash so they put me back on the shelf. Seconds later a widow with an eight-year-old daughter and two boys of six and seven put me in her shopping trolley. She had a menagerie of abandoned children, sometimes as many as ten within her crowded house. Often five of us were crammed into one room. I thought I was back in the Spirit world, with so many children like me, who came for a week or two, and then disappeared into another world.

I had become a mass murderer by the time I left my second family, killing off in my head all the children that had come and gone, sharing my room for a month or two. I didn't even know you were meant to mourn. Instead I just wished I was dead too and roaming again in the heavens with my other Spirit friends. But it's too late. I've got what I wished for – a successful rebirth.

I arrive just in time for Santa again. I am special. I am the permanent youngest. I stay three and a half years, long enough to call some one Mummy. I am the pride and glory of my new sister Sally. I'm her new coloured fuzzy doll. Our mum never has time to look after us all, so Sally has almost full custody of me. She takes me out for walks in her wicker basket perched upon her bicycle handlebars. We paint the streets of Bristol in zebra fashion, courting so much attention that Sally becomes the local entrepreneur.

Passers-by stop and stare. "That's a lovely native doll you have there, can I have a look?" Sometimes they put their hand in my hair and then jump with fright, screaming, "Golly gumdrops, it's alive."

"It's my baby sister, Pauline," Sally protests.

"You horrid child, don't tell lies," and off they'd walk in a huff.

The local children try to make us cry by making monkey noises and calling us smelly baboons. But Sally puts a stop to this. She introduces me as her new walky-talky native doll, and charges them four gob stoppers, six black jacks, or a bag of pineapple chunks for a quick peek.

I develop a sweet tooth and rapidly grow too big for the bicycle basket. By the age of three, I'm transferred into a red wheelbarrow, and we earn threepenny bits and sixpences by letting children push me up and down a nearby lane. Sometimes we get half a crown when Sally takes a gang on a guided tour to parade me through White Ladies Road and up Black Boy Hill.

Sally saves up the money to buy us second-hand toys that our mum can't afford. I fall in love with a big white smiling baby doll, with huge eyes that roll. Sally buys it from the charity shop for my fourth birthday. Her loose golden curls and her pink blossom cheeks enchant me. She looks just like the angels in my Bible picture book. I name her Gabriel and take her out with me on the wheelbarrow trips.

One Saturday afternoon I have a terrible shock. A lady who lives in our Lane stops all three of us outside our house and says: "What an extraordinary sight. Can I take a picture?"

The red and white lady arranges us. Tells us to smile. Clicks her camera. Then hands me a piece of stiff paper and says: "Its magic, count to a hundred." I get lost after ten, and so she tells me to pull the tab, and gently peel back the cover of the photo. Excitedly, I rip it off and something strange begins to happen.

Sally and Gabriel grow lighter and lighter and I remain as dark as the night. I scream and throw Gabriel and the picture to the ground. Sally grabs the doll and shoves a gobstopper in my mouth. The lady puts her hand in her pocket and pulls a shilling out for my sister and says: "Here, take this, buy her a gollywog. She'll probably prefer that instead."

Sally never pushes me in the barrow again. She says I'm too big and instead I have to walk and push Gabriel in it if I want to play with her. She tells me to start growing up and sends me home that day. I sulk in my bedroom, then pull out some of Gabriel's hair and, with my pink brush, comb and mirror set, place her golden locks over my black corkscrews. It makes me happy until I catch sight of myself. There isn't enough hair to make me blonde.

"Why can't I be like Gabriel," I cry. I throw Gabriel under my bed and pull all the stuffing out of a new teddy bear.

I begin to scream.

"Be quiet up there," Mummy shouts back.

And I throw myself into a heap and wail.

A gust of wind blows the curtains, knocking Paddington Bear and Winnie the Pooh off the windowsill. I jump up, wipe my face with my sleeve and look up at the window. Blowing in are tiny sparkles, just like the sparklers from bonfire night. Coloured fairy lights shine through the window. Then I hear a whisper: "Pauline, Pauline follow me," and the sparkles dance in front of my face.

"What's your name?" Nobody answers and the colours keep on flickering.

"Tell me your name now. If you don't, I won't play with you." My whole bedroom fills up with sparkles.

"Meany. I'll call you Sparky and see how you like that." I let the sparkles jump all over my hands, and follow them into the bathroom.

I climb into the toilet, open the bottle of bleach beside the toilet pan and pour it all over me. I scream and Sally comes running in, yanks the bottle from my hands and begins to scream too. Mummy rescues us by throwing us under the bath tap, and shouts: "You're becoming unmanageable, too much of a handful for our Sally."

I think they don't want me anymore because I don't turn white. Mummy knows how to make everything else white, except me. When I plead with her, she says it's impossible. But I don't believe her. I scrub my skin, chalk myself, dip my hands and face in flour. Sally becomes angrier with me, my brothers laugh, and Mummy slaps me.

Soon after, I say goodbye as Mummy, my sister and brothers stand like soldiers outside our house. I think they're playing a game. I try to find a space between their bodies to run back inside. But Mummy looks like a giant guarding the door, and nobody opens their legs for me to crawl back home.

"Bye bye, Pauline. We love you. We'll all be thinking of you," Mummy shrieks.

"What's thinking, Sally?" I ask desperately.

Sally squeezes my hand when I leave her, tears roller-coasting down her cheeks. I feel like I am holding an ice-lolly that is just about to fall off its stick. Mummy's and my brothers' faces squash into one and everything becomes a blur. I watch their hands waving and know this is what people do when they say goodbye. I try my hardest to make them all go upstairs to heaven so I don't have to think of them anymore.

I used to think my life began at four and a half, and now I know why. Everyone I had ever met before then had died. Dead meant people who came into my life, then disappeared, and who I never saw again.

2

I say hello to a lady called Mrs Stark; she has short brown wavy hair, and a red Mini. I have a social worker now instead of a mummy. We travel down huge roads with thousands of tiny moving houses passing us by. People wave at me, and I wave goodbye back to them. I notice that they all look white, and I wonder what they have eaten to look like Gabriel, my dead family, and Mrs Stark.

I want to leap out of my seat and be back in my barrow with the other kids pushing me down a muddy track screaming: "Choc Ice for sale, Choc Ice for sale."

I have a huge lump inside my throat, and I can't swallow. It hurts so much that I think I'm going to die. I hold onto Gabriel sprawled across my lap, wishing we'd wake up to Sally waiting to piggyback us down to breakfast.

Then I am very brave and ask: "Where are we going?"

Mrs Stark looks at me for the first time, smiles sweetly and replies, "I'm taking you to Dr Barnardo's."

"But I'm not sick," I protest. "Sick people go to the doctor. I'm not sick, honest. Can I go back home now?"

"I am taking you home to a beautiful village in Essex, Pauline. Be quiet so I don't lose the way."

I look down at my hands and wonder if I have a disease.

They are chocolate brown on one side and a dirty white on the other. Maybe this doctor is going to cure me and make me all white. He'll make my mummy, my sister and two brothers come back to life, and I can go back home. And then everything will be all right.

Mrs Stark and I don't speak again until we arrive outside a black iron gate, with a huge red brick wall. She stops driving, pulls out a picture book, tugs my hand and says: "You have to help me find the back gate."

She points to the picture book and says: "We have to follow the red brick wall. You call out when you see some apple and pear trees, and then we'll be at the back gate."

"Can I eat the apples?"

"We'll have to ask your new house parents that."

"Will my new parents look like houses?"

"Let's wait and see, Pauline."

When we drive past the apples and pears a big gap appears and Mrs Stark stops suddenly.

"You're supposed to be watching out for me, Pauline. Here we are." She drives through the gap, and I sit glued to my seat, watching big boys and girls leap over fences and chase after each other.

"Come on, Pauline, let's find your new home."

I take hold of my doll Gabriel, and Mrs Stark takes my hand and drags me along the tarmac. She points out the food stores, the dentist and the junior school. A big boy with orange hair comes running up and says: "Are you new?"

"Yes, do you know where Cross Cottage is?" replies Mrs Stark.

He points towards a large patch of grass. "It's over there, the one with the pink door."

"Thank you very much," she replies. "Look over there, Pauline, that must be the clock tower."

I see a tall house painted in mustard and brown, with a big clock perched high up on a tower. I hear the clock dong five times, and then see lots of painted doors fly open and people shouting across the green: "Teatime!" And all the children playing on the grass run off into their homes. I pull at Mrs Stark's red woollen coat sleeve and say: "Take me home. Why can't I live with my mummy?"

"You're too young to understand," she replies. So I never ask again. "Look, here it is, Cross Cottage. Isn't it pretty? Look at the roses on the front lawn," Mrs Stark points out.

I trip up over my shoelaces just before we arrive outside the front door. Lots of people run around me, and I can see strange faces staring into my eyes. "Is the little 'un okay?" somebody asks. I begin to cry.

"I think it's best she's put to bed, she's had a long day," Mrs Stark replies. A big man picks me up and takes me inside, up some stairs and tucks me up in bed. I fall asleep and dream of being left on hospital steps, crying in tune to the deafening sounds of feet passing by. Next I am left in a dustbin with the lid on, struggling for air until a moon-like face peers in and gently picks me up. I call out to my friend Jack: "Please help me find a mummy and daddy." He takes my hand and helps me climb up his beanstalk. "Stay here," he whispers. And I wait until he returns. "Tomorrow," he whispers. But a mummy and daddy never come.

I call: "Pinocchio, Pinocchio," and ask him to take me for an adventure in a big fish's tummy, but he doesn't hear me.

Sparkles ignite all over my bed and someone is tugging at my head. I feel like I am being sucked out of my body. I hold my breath with fear, but before I can cling onto my sheets, Sparky is showing me how to play with him. He teaches me to leave my body and rise above it by hovering over me until I have the courage to float up to his coloured lights.

He holds my hand when I first start flying and takes me as high as my bedroom ceiling. I rise out of my body on my own and find some new friends. I make contact with other young sad souls who yearn to be back in the Spirit world too. There are as many as six abreast holding hands as we fly above the rooftops into the dark blue sky. I can't see any of them, but when I hear the sound of chattering teeth, I stretch out my arms and reach for someone's hand. We fly above the clouds side by side with all the wild birds. We kaleidoscope among the watery stars, and follow their bright trails. We play underneath the big dipper, helter-skeltering all the way back down to our beds when we fall off. Other times we zigzag through the heavens in hope of meeting the gods.

It is here I first make friends with the Angels. They look like candyfloss, pink, yellow and white, all fluffy with bright light surrounding them. I always know when I'm near them because a soft gust of air hugs my skin, and I tingle deep inside.

I wonder if going to live with the Angels could be better than living in my new home.

"Can you make me dead? " I ask.

"Why do you want to be dead, Pauline?" the Angels inquire.

"So I can begin a new life in heaven with you and all my dead friends."

"One day you'll be an Angel just like us," they reply.

"I want to be an Angel now."

"Patience, Pauline, patience."

"If I die now why can't I come and live in heaven?"

"It's not your turn, Pauline."

When I stop flying high in the skies I dream of falling.

I'm on the tops of trees in the jungle, a mountain crag, and when I fall from a skyscraper I reach up for Sally,

Mummy and my two brothers to grab me. "Watch out," they all shout.

I wake up with a jolt, and Mrs Stark has gone. I know I'm never going back to my old family and that Cross Cottage is my new home.

Gabriel is lying face down on the floor. I have finally managed to kill her off too.

In my new room are four beds, four rugs, four chairs, a chest of drawers.

Heidi and Inez are my new friends. I am the baby once again. Inez is seven, with iron stitches joining all her teeth. The boys call her Bugs Bunny. Heidi is almost nine. She wears two strawberry pigtails, and pulls the ribbons out of her hair as soon as she leaves the house. Pippa is the oldest at twelve so she has her own room. She is very tall and walks with her shoulders hunched up to her ears, and has beautiful pink skin. Next-door are the boys – Keith, Simon and Paul. Keith is six, has thick brown hair that hides his Dumbo ears. Paul is six too, has large blue eyes, yellow hair and sucks his thumb. Simon is seven and has lots of spots on his face.

On the other side of my room sleeps my new house parents, Aunty Claire and Uncle Boris. Their son Nathan is eleven years old, and has his own room by the stairs at the end of the landing. He speaks with a stutter and everyone says he is very slow. Aunty Morag sleeps next door to Aunty Claire and Uncle Boris.

When Nathan first meets me, he screams, points to a scab on his knee and asks: "Mum, will I go the same colour as Pauline?"

Laughing, she says: "We're all the same, and you're not to mention Pauline's colour again," but Nathan runs off shouting,

"Yuck, I've caught the lurgy." I soon forget I'm different, because Aunty Claire reminds me that we are all the same whenever I try to pick my skin. "We all bleed red," she tells the other children in the Cottage when they call me names. I think Dr Barnardo's has cured my disease.

We have two Red Setters, Duke and Duchess, a Persian cat called Milo, another cat called Tabby, a parrot, budgie, fishes, hamsters and rabbits. There's a boot room by the back door, toilets, a utility room, kitchen, pantry, bathroom, playroom, and a dining room and staff room by the front door.

Aunty Claire is from the Lake District. She is very proud and neat. She wears knee-high white patent boots, skirts above her knees and crew neck jumpers. She tells me: "You have the best house parents in the Village, the best Cottage and the best garden." Her husband is a German Jew. He sits at the head of the dining-room table every mealtime, smoking Old Holborn tobacco and hiding behind a volcano of newspapers. Aunty Claire says one day he will erupt into a huge fire if he keeps on smoking while reading and eating at the table. He should think himself lucky he didn't die in the gas chambers.

Uncle Boris is unlike other house fathers because he's not allowed to work inside the Village as he is not a Christian. So he is like a proper dad and goes out to work every day at a Kodak camera firm. And we get extra treats like a colour television, and paper chase rides in posh new cars.

He speaks funny words that nobody can understand. He says "nein" instead of no, "ya" instead of yes, and calls all the children "kinder" and says we live on the "kinder" green. He tells us stories of coming to England on the "Kinder Transport Scheme". Tears wash his eyes every time he describes having to leave his mum, dad, aunts, and uncles behind in Germany to come and live in a home for Jewish children. He always ends by saying "Oy vey".

Aunty Morag is fat, a good cook, cries in the pantry, and has hair down to her bottom when she loosens it from a French pleat piled up high on her head.

When she is happy we play with her tin of buttons, and hundreds of small picture baby books. In the evening she lets one of us hold her skein of wool while she hypnotises us as she makes it into a big fat ball. If we're lucky she shows us how to play cats' cradle and how to make a cup and saucer by wrapping wool around our hands and doing gymnastics with our fingers.

My Cottage is one of many. It lives on the kinder green, along with twenty others, which surround a large patch of green grass. Outside my front door is a sandpit and two gigantic conker trees. I watch in awe when the big children throw sticks up into the trees and scream when green prickly things fall down.

"Climb up," someone shouts. And a boy runs up the tree trunk like a squirrel and then swings from branch to branch like a monkey. "Shake the tree," the children roar up to him. He shakes and more conkers fall to the ground.

"It's a cheezer," I hear someone holler.

I run outside to taste one that has landed near my front door. It is flat, smooth and shiny on one side and round on the other. I bite into it, and spit it out when I realise it doesn't taste like the Dairy Lea cheese wrapped in silver paper that we get for tea. I wonder if I soak them in vinegar and roast them in the oven like Aunty Morag has told me if they will taste like real cheese.

Nathan teaches me the art of conkering. "Put a nail

through the centre, thread a bootlace through the hole and tie a knot so it stays on. Find someone who has a ninety-niner to compete with. Always aim for the fingers, so the other person drops it. Then you can do stampseys. And then yours will be a one hundreder. Look, just like this."

Nathan whacks my knuckles and before I can let out a howl, he's stamping all over my precious conker that I've clung onto for one whole day.

He always has a winning conker everyone wants to defeat. Most of the young kids are jealous of him. They call Nathan a big baby because he is eleven years old and still plays with conkers.

On the other side of the green are swings, a seesaw and a roundabout. I watch the big boys and girls sit on the swings and hurl themselves over the bar. Other children are playing cricket and rounders.

A fountain spurts water all day and in the summer we often cool ourselves off under its pelting spray. The red brick church, where we stand in crocodile line every Sunday waiting to enter, is on the edge of the kinder green. And the clock tower ding-dongs every hour.

There is also a big house where children in wheelchairs play outside all day long, sometimes making funny noises. There is a sports green too – huge, with lots more Cottages, and where we hold sports days and football matches. It's closer to the hospital, the nursery school, the Cottages where the babies live, and the adventure playground.

There is also a memorial green where there are more Cottages by the swimming pool, laundry and the clothes store. It is where Dr Barnardo has been turned into black stone.

I have moved from a matchbox house on a tiny street to an enormous Legoland with hundreds of children like me, all without mummies and daddies. I settle in a week, forgetting all about my dead family and the wheelbarrow. I have become enchanted by my new home.

I am different from the other girls in my Cottage. I play outside and get my clothes dirty. Often they are so muddy that Aunty Morag threatens to throw me fully clothed into the bath, but she never does.

By day seven, Aunty Claire christens me Minstrel. At first it's a joke, but it soon sticks like mud and everyone in my new family calls me that. I almost forget my name.

"It's The Black and White Minstrel Show," Aunty Claire cackles. Everyone laughs and Aunty Claire picks me up, puts me on her lap and says: "Who's a beautiful Minstrel?"

Every time the whole family watches the show on television on Saturday afternoons, someone shouts out: "Look! They look just like Pauline." I walk up to the wooden box and stare at six men with wide white eyes and big fat painted white lips in bowler hats and suits. Everyone laughs and Aunty Morag, says: "We'll have to send you off to tap-dancing lessons soon."

Nathan calls me a Nig Nog and says I look like the funny men on the television even though Aunty Morag tells him off and says he's not to say that word again.

I begin to sulk at home and play on my own, and I'm teased even more. When I'm indoors I play with Sparky under my bed so nobody can see my special friend and at night I visit the Angels. Heidi and Inez complain to the Aunties that it's impossible for them to sleep because I often sleepwalk and talk nonsense in my sleep. They both lean over my bed, pull my sheets back and shout: "You've got one more chance or else!"

During my first few months at the Village, I trip over all the time. I don't mind because I'm flying in the skies with the Angels, but Aunty Claire and Aunty Morag decide something must be wrong with me, and I'm packed off to hospital in London for a brain scan. A silly man makes me a strawberry milkshake with water, and says to drink it all up. I ask for some milk, but Aunty Claire says I should do as I am told. I gulp it down, and in the next moment I'm falling asleep on her lap. I wake up in a bed, with the silly man tapping cutlery on my head, and flashing big bright lights before my eyes.

He says, "As you've been such a good girl, you can go home now," and gives me a big bag of sweets.

"You're not to eat them until you've had your tea," says Aunty Claire. So I share them with everybody when I arrive home. Heidi and Inez are my best friends now, and nobody ever mentions my hospital visit again.

A week later I have an accident. I've gone visiting my Angels and Spirit friends, and when it's time for me to come back I get stuck.

My body will not move. I am paralysed in mid-air. I stare down at myself lying in bed, trying to call my name. But I can't speak. I try to scream out aloud, and still no sound will come out of my mouth. I look at myself with terror not knowing what to do, and then a rainbow begins to flash all over me and I am sucked back into my body in seconds.

I sit bolt upright in bed and scream the house down for Sparky. Aunty Morag comes running in. Heidi and Inez are furious. I've woken them up out of their sleep. "Get her out of here, she's giving us nightmares," Heidi shouts.

"Shut up and don't be so insensitive," Aunty Morag shouts back. "Minstrel can't help it if she has nightmares."

In the morning Heidi and Inez lean over my bed like

giraffes and shout at me again.

"We can't sleep because of you, you stupid overgrown baby," says Inez.

"You've blown your last chance," says Heidi.

"Yeah, we're sending you off to Coventry for your punishment." I pack my toys in my pillowcase and wait by the front door for my social worker, Mrs Stark, to come and take me away.

"What are you doing, Minstrel?" asks Aunty Claire.

"I'm waiting to go to Coventry." She laughs and walks off. When Heidi and Inez finish breakfast, I ask what time I'll be leaving, but they pretend not to hear me and run off giggling. I never go to Coventry, but Heidi and Inez stop talking to me so I'm without friends for a while. They also pick on Nathan because he's the house parents' son, teasing him by saying: "You've got a screw loose just like Minstrel." So Nathan and I play together.

I'm too scared to play with the Angels and Sparky for a while, and so I begin to make new friends. Minstrel plays indoors and Pauline plays outside.

3

Aunty Morag says that the people of Timbuktu can hear me when I scream the house down every morning before I go to nursery school. She brushes my hair until my head feels as if it's caught fire. Then with her fat hands she ties a pink ribbon around it. The ribbon is so tight, that I can't feel my feet anymore, and I can feel Sparky pulling me up towards the sky.

"Minstrel," Aunty Morag screams, "haven't you learnt to dress yourself properly yet?" I land back on the ground, wondering if my head will explode. My ears are hot from all the nagging.

"Why can't I have rags in my hair like Heidi and Inez?"

"You've got curls already, stupid. Now put on your socks and slippers before you eat breakfast."

Keith, Paul and I are the three youngest. Every morning after breakfast we are sent off to do paper toilet.

Paul gasps: "Just push. Are you pushing? Keep on pushing. It's coming, Aunty. I've been to paper toilet," he calls aloud.

Aunty Morag comes running into the toilets and asks if she can see his pooh. She checks he's been and then pulls the chain.

"What about you, Minstrel, have you been?"

"I don't know?"

"What do you mean, you don't know?"

"I'm stuck."

"Stuck, why on earth you should be constipated, you stuffed yourself with prunes last night at suppertime."

I start crying. I'm stuck in the toilet and can't pull myself out to show her whether I've been or not.

She laughs so loud that everyone comes running in, but she slams the door in their faces and pulls me out. My bottom is wet and I beg Aunty Morag not to send me to paper toilet anymore. She ignores me and escorts me off to paper toilet the next day.

Sometimes it's so hard to go toilet after breakfast that I make the pan look like raspberry ripple ice cream. My bottom bleeds and feels as if it's caught the pins and needles disease. Other days we ask the older kids to go for us, and then hold our noses and shout together: "Aunty, we've been to paper toilet." One of the Aunties arrives a few minutes later, checks the pooh and says well done. And then we're all dragged off to school for the day.

On my first day at my new nursery school we walk across the big sports green and past the adventure playground. I see someone who looks like the black and white tap-dancing men on the television. I get scared and stop and stare. "Look Aunty, there's a Minstrel," I point.

He spits at me and shouts: "Nig Nog," and runs off.

Aunty says: " Never point, it's rude and it upsets people."

On my second day I play with a transistor. It's lying on the floor and I can hear it crackling. I think Sparky has come to play with me again. I want to see Sparky so I pull it apart and find red and green veins attached to a blue battery. A teacher hurriedly runs up to me and pulls it out of my hands.

"What are you doing, Pauline?"

"I'm playing with Sparky. Look, he's speaking to me."

"Who is Sparky?"

"My special friend."

She pulls the transistor from my hand and says: "You're not in a zoo. This is a proper nursery school with well-mannered children."

I throw plasticine at the wall and jump over the cardboard boxes on the floor. Some of the smaller children cry and the ones as big as me try to hide behind the toys.

"I'm sending you home, Pauline Charles. And tomorrow leave your monkey habits at Cross Cottage."

Aunty Morag comes to collect me. She teases me and says if I'm not careful I'll grow up to be a tomboy, and I should start playing with dolls in the nursery. She squashes my hand all the way home, and gives me an old transistor to play with for the rest of the day. I take it upstairs to my bedroom, but can't understand why Sparky won't talk to me anymore.

The next day Aunty Morag puts two ribbons in my hair and dresses me in a bright yellow dress. "What a lovely pretty girl you are. Now make sure you play with dolls today at school, like proper little girls do. And remember to smile, you're having your picture taken today." The ribbons in my hair are even tighter today so I end up having a smile ironed all over my face. I scream in front of the camera, but the man ignores me and makes a big flash.

The next girl screams too. And so we become best friends. Her name is Elizabeth. She has strawberry-coloured pigtails just like Heidi and lives in Swaddling Cottage on the memorial green. We play I'm the King of the Castle and You're the Dirty Rascal and take turns clambering up to the top of a climbing frame to be King. Elizabeth makes a crown out of sticks and leaves; mine is made from egg boxes and pipe cleaners. We paint our hands red and then hold hands tight so that we can become blood sisters. We try to wear the same clothes to school, and the teachers call us the chalk and cheese sisters.

Every day after lunch the teachers put all the children down to sleep. Elizabeth and I whisper to each other about being Kings and Queens and living in a castle. The horrible teacher who stole my transistor comes scuttling up and says: "It's Pauline again. I might have guessed, and Elizabeth too. Come on you two, get up. You're disturbing everyone else." She puts us into a room on the floor beside some smelly shoes. "Here, maybe this will help you sleep." She gives us each a boiled sweet and plays "A Spoonful of Sugar Makes the Medicine Go Down" on the record player. I fall asleep with sugar drizzling down my throat.

We chat every snooze time until the teacher puts us to bed in the cheesy room, gives us a sweet and plays the same song to make us sleep.

One afternoon I ask, "Elizabeth, do you want to visit the Angels with me?"

"Yes, please." So we hold hands and fall asleep, hoping to float up into the clouds. When we wake up, Elizabeth says: "I couldn't see the Angels." I promise her the next time it will really really work. It never does with her and she begins to get angry with me and says she'll stop being my friend if I don't stop telling porky pies.

One day Elizabeth arrives at nursery school and announces: "I'm leaving."

"No, you can't," I shout back

"Yes, I can, I'm leaving next week."

"No, No, No!" And I stampede around the playground.

"I can't play with you anymore."

"But you're my best friend."

21

"I can't be your best friend anymore."

I try to pull at Elizabeth's hand but she pulls it away and looks at it.

"My new mummy says I can't have a coloured sister. She says I'm different from you."

"But we share everything."

"Not now. I'm leaving."

"I want a new mummy and daddy. Can I come too?"

"I did ask, but they said I'll forget you and all my friends in a week, and everything will be all right."

I blink, splashing my face with tears. "Can I visit?"

"No. My new mummy says I have to start a new life and put Dr Barnardos behind me."

That afternoon after lunch, the boiled sweet gets stuck in my throat and I know I don't want to say goodbye to anyone else. When Elizabeth doesn't turn up for a week and nobody mentions her name, I know I have managed to kill her off. I sleep in the cheesy room on my own after that and hide the sweets in the smelly shoes. I'm back flying with the Angels in the daylight, and Sparky comes to visit me too. He makes a noise by rocking me in my sleep. He pulls me up to play with him. I bump into the wall and trip over the carpet. The teachers catch me sleepwalking around the room. They complain about me to my house parents and they all agree that I am most probably ready for big school.

4

Children should be seen and not heard. There is an awkward silence at the breakfast table. Inez is treading on my foot under the table and I'm trying my hardest not to yelp. Her foot is saying, ugh yuck, the white of the egg is all runny. I drop my egg into my lap, hoping that the Angels or Sparky will eat it for me. The others are forcing tiny bits of egg between their lips from the tips of their teaspoons. Just as Nathan is about to tell tales on me about my egg, Aunty Claire tells Heidi she has to hold my hand and take me to my new school every morning before she runs upstairs to junior school.

Heidi protests. "It's only across the lane. She's six, for godsake."

"I don't care, you're to hold her hand," says Aunty Claire. "And only speak when you're spoken to."

"But look, she's a mess."

"Minstrel," Aunty Morag shouts, "leave the table now." Uncle Boris is sitting at the head of the table behind his huge newspaper. He lowers it, blows a puff of smoke and winks at me. And I know he understands that I can't eat my runny eggs.

"Stop dawdling. You've got egg yolk all over your new

clean clothes," Aunty Morag bellows. Inez glares at me and Nathan tries to trip me up. Everyone is jealous of me because I don't have to eat the egg.

Keith and Paul both join me in the toilets. I can hear them squirting out their pooh and Aunty complaining about them having the runs. I have to get Nathan to go for me, and he's got the runs too. Aunty Morag thinks I'm nervous about my first day at big school, and gives me a cuddle.

I wait for Heidi in the boot room. She grabs at me grudgingly and I trip over all the shoes. She pays me sixpence to let go of her hand as soon as the back door is shut. I take the sixpence and hide it in my satchel. But once we're at the backyard gate I'm scared. I can see all the big boys in the playground playing aeroplanes, bumper cars and British bulldogs. Heidi pushes me through the gate and I snatch at her arm and hold on tight.

"Let go! Don't go showing me up." She shakes me off and I land head-first in a puddle, my knees and hands scratched. I begin to cry.

"Stop showing me up," she screams again. Then she yanks me out of the puddle and tries to squeeze the rainwater out of my green pinafore and blazer. I cry some more, and refuse to take one more step towards. I don't make it to big school on my first day.

The next day Heidi says sorry, and promises that I can hold on to her hand for as long as I like. But I'm more scared than yesterday. I ask her for a fireman's hug, but she says we're not at home now, and we have to behave like big girls when we're outside. It's over fifty steps from our back door to the school playground. I count and hold my breath, and I skate on the frost that iced up last night. Heidi shakes me off as soon as we reach the playground. I slip but manage to grab at her bag.

I look up and see lots of big windows staring down at

me. There are grey bricks, and a door which says Primary and another which says Junior. There are lots of children dressed in green, with scarves and berets, clambering over rusty railings which run along the front of the school.

A whistle is blown. "Don't follow me, babies go downstairs," Heidi orders. "I'll meet you by these railings at home time. This is your teacher, Mrs Bright."

Mrs Bright looks like a green runner bean with ginger hair. In the classroom she announces that we have a new girl today from Cross Cottage. Nobody is interested. I'm shoved into a Wendy house and play doctor and nurses all day with two girls who joined the school the week before.

At playtime one of the big boys calls out: "Mrs Bright?"

She puts out her cigarette and turns around, looking startled.

"Yes?"

He says: "Have you had a fright."

"No. Now go and play somewhere else," she scowls.

"Look at your yellow fingers. Mrs Bright must have had a fright."

She pushes her hands in her coat pocket, and says: "That's enough of this nonsense."

"In the middle of the night," the skinny boy continues to chant.

"Now that would be a frightful sight," answers Mrs Bright.

"Oh look, I can see your ghost eating toast, halfway up a lamp post," he replies, and then runs off giggling. During playtime, one by one a big child comes up to her, asks the same questions and then runs off laughing.

On my third day at school, I ask; "Mrs Bright, why do the big children ask if you have had a fright, in the middle of the night?"

"You impetuous child. I'll teach you not to copy the big children." She frog-marches me off to the washrooms and lathers my mouth out with carbolic soap. It slides all over my tongue and gets stuck in my teeth. I feel sick every time I swallow.

I wait until I grow big like Heidi, before I ask her the questions again. And I make sure she never washes my mouth out. I begin to enjoy my new big school; we play all day with cardboard boxes, squeezy bottles and glue. And then overnight, I start to do big kid things like learning to write my full name and address and adding up sums.

"Can't you write your name, Pauline Charles? Six years old, whatever next?" asks Mrs Bright.

"I can," and pick up the crayon in my left hand.

"You wicked child. Daughter of the Devil, don't ever let me see you use your left hand again."

"Yes, Aunty Claire."

"A daydreamer too," she yells. And turns to the rest of the class and orders: "Stop this laughter now everyone, before I wash all your mouths out with carbolic soap. Pauline, come to the front of the class."

I walk up to Mrs Bright, not knowing what she wants me to do.

"Turn around with your back to the class. Now put your left hand behind your back. This is what will happen if I catch any of you writing with your left hand."

I hear the whole class gasp and stop breathing as she tapes my hand to my back. She sends me to a desk at the back of the classroom and then instructs us to copy out lines all day. Mrs Bright breaks five pieces of chalk as she carves "I must always write with my right hand or burn in hell" into the blackboard.

The classroom goes foggy and my eyes spill out over my

desk. Sparky appears dancing all over the paper. He takes my right hand and makes me write. I press so hard that the crayons keep on snapping and Mrs Bright screams that she will get the devil out of me even if it kills her. Sparky keeps on breaking my crayons, and I stare at the blackboard until I can go home.

Aunty Morag says it's for the best, that I have to keep on trying to use my right hand, and then everything will be all right.

But it isn't true what Aunty Morag promises me. When I learn to write my name with my right hand, Mrs Bright still shouts at me and complains about my scruffy handwriting. But I don't care anymore because I can write my name in full with my new hand. Sometimes I don't know what to do with my new pair of hands. It's as if my two hands can't think together anymore and things go all wobbly and wrong. Nobody will play two balls with me in the backyard because I'm always dropping the balls. The Aunties and my teacher say I'm a slow learner and Heidi and Inez say I suffer from clumsyitus. I think my left hand is turning into the devil, so I try pulling it off. When that doesn't work, I just let Sparky help me with my writing, and put up with being told off whenever he decides to tear pages out of my exercise book.

My favourite lesson is needlework. We keep all our cross-stitching and patchwork in shoeboxes. Our needlework teacher, Mrs Hopper, looks like a big rabbit. She has a bun on top of her head and whiskers sprouting all over her chin. She sits behind a table and demonstrates all the different stitches she wants us to try. Everyone knows she sits with her legs wide open wearing old-fashioned bloomers. So one by one we drop our shoeboxes to the floor, jump down to pick them up and have a quick look up her large flowing skirt. She is always wearing bloomers with big red spots. Once we've seen the bloomers we have a quick giggle and sit back at our desk for the next person to have a look. Mrs Hopper says she can't understand why people are so careless in her class. We protest out aloud, telling her how much we love blanket and herringbone stitch, and promise to be more careful with our shoeboxes.

When I'm seven I move upstairs to Junior school with all the big children. Heidi has joined Pippa's secondary school which is outside of the village. Nathan is at special school, Keith and Paul are in the year above me, Simon and Inez are in the second year at junior school.

My new teacher is called Mrs Swift. She is very small, talks very fast and everyone warns you not to cross her path. She has purple hair and wears her glasses dangling around her neck. She tells us that we must all be an example to the younger ones downstairs. She is very strict, and allows no talking, whispering or chewing in her classroom. If she catches you talking, she sends you home with a hundred lines – "I must not talk in class". If you say words like "stroppy" she scrubs your mouth out with soap, just like Mrs Bright. If you answer back she gives you the ruler across your knuckles, and if you are really naughty she whacks you on the bottom with a slipper. If that doesn't work you're sent to the headmaster for the cane.

So we are all scared of her. I wish for the weekend to come because there is nobody younger than me at home I have to be a good example to. I can be the baby and play peep behind the curtain and hide and seek. My favourite hiding place is the laundry basket. On Fridays it's always full of warm clean sheets. Aunty Morag says I should find somewhere else to hide because one day I'll get carted off to the laundry and put into a giant washing machine to be spun and dried. It sounds like a great adventure, so I try my hardest not to be found. Every Monday morning Sparky and I play hide and seek in secret underneath the dirty sheets, but Nathan always seems to find us. He promises not to tell that he has seen me speaking to the sheets and pillowcases as long as I let him join in. He tickles me in the basket, ties me up in the sheets, and puts a pillowcase over my head. He sits on top of the basket and keeps me captive until he can feel me struggling for air. And then he lets me out and says this is our little secret, quick, run before we get caught.

5

It's always a rush to leave the Cottage when Uncle Boris takes us on an outing at weekends. While us younger ones struggle to get ready, the older ones climb all over us in the boot room, arguing over which Wellington boots belong to who. Uncle Boris always screams at high volume for us to shut up and hurry up. And after a few tears and harsh words between us eight kids, we manage to arrive in one piece in the lounge, bundled up in anoraks and scarves, with some of us wearing a pair of two left or two right boots.

"Sitzen," Uncle Boris orders. And we all fall like dominoes, including our two Aunties, into armchairs, wondering what an earth he is going to make us do next. In the stern silence, even the two dogs, Duke and Duchess, know not to bark. At this point in the ritual, I always get the itches and somehow manage to fall off the bit of sofa that Heidi and Nathan have kindly allocated me. The adults' faces freeze and the two dogs sniff at me. Then the signal, and Uncle Boris is out of his seat like a Jack in a Box for the drive to the forest. As we file out of the Cottage into the minibus, Aunty Claire mutters, "I told you the Germans are all mad."

Ten minutes later, we arrive at the forest. It's cold, the leaves squelch and the trees look like skeletons hanging in the sky. Uncle Boris takes the boys and the dogs and I'm left with the Aunties, Heidi, Inez and Pippa. Before parting, Uncle Boris swaps a bag of white stones for a bag of sandwiches with Aunty Claire.

She scowls: "Not another one of your German eccentricities."

"What is German electricity, Aunty Claire?" I ask.

Aunty ignores me, and thrusts the bag of stones into her pocket.

We walk off into the forest, singing songs. Pippa walks on ahead and gets stuck in some bog. Aunty Morag manages to pull her out, but one of her boots gets left behind. So Pippa sulks all afternoon, limping slowly behind while Inez, Heidi and I run off to find trees to climb. Heidi picks me up and sits me on her broad shoulders. Inez climbs up a tree and hangs her arms down towards me. "Hold on tight," she calls down, and pulls me up off Heidi's shoulders.

I catch her hands and swing my legs out to help me find a branch.

"Ouch, it hurts." I've landed on a branch sticking into my legs.

"Bring her down right now," Aunty Claire screams up at us.

But Heidi and Inez are already sitting high in the sky with my Angel friends, while I'm bawling out aloud: "I want to come down now."

And then it's time to go home. Half an hour has passed and we still can't find the minibus. Pippa says she doesn't want to go home anyway, she'd rather live in the forest with the trees. Aunty Claire says that's okay as long as she is willing to share her bed with foxes, snakes and all the ghosts that will come to haunt her. It begins to get dark, and my two Aunties have a look on their faces I've not seen before.

Heidi pulls a torch out of her anorak and says: "Follow me, I'm a good Girl Guide."

It makes the Aunties laugh and off we follow.

"Look, Aunty Claire, look, there's some white stones," Heidi points out. Aunty Morag says they must belong to Uncle Boris, let's see if there are any more. And so we all begin to look and there are lots of white stones everywhere. We follow them, Heidi leading us with her torch. And suddenly we see some bright lights flashing in mid-air. Heidi shouts: "Quick, let's run, it's a ghost coming to spook us." As she turns, Duke and Duchess come running up and jump all over us, licking our faces. The boys and Uncle Boris are laughing.

"I'm not so mad after all. I bet you didn't use your stones?" Uncle Boris says. "You're the dumb kopfs," he teases.

"Take us home, we're all cold from being lost in the forest," Aunty Claire fumes. So we go home with all the adults in a bad mood.

That night we're sent to bed earlier than usual. Uncle Boris catches some of us talking in bed. He calls out for Paul, Keith, Inez and I to come out on to the landing and tells us to stand with our faces to the wall and hands on our heads. "Now stop talking."

We do for five minutes, but when Nathan comes up to bed he throws a slipper at me. I throw it back. It misses and hits Duke who is sleeping on the landing. Duke begins to bark and Uncle Boris comes storming upstairs:

"Right, that's it, all four of you in bed early for a week. And you can all stay out here for another fifteen minutes."

Inez tells tales and say's it's all my fault. So the next night I am the only one who is made to go to bed early. When Paul comes up to bed, we begin talking to each other from our different rooms and we both get caught again. So again Uncle Boris puts us on the landing, this time at opposite ends so we can't see each other. I end up near Nathan's room.

He whispers: "Minstrel," and I ignore him. His hand pulls me into his bedroom. Then there are footsteps on the stairs, so he pushes me back out. I stand with my hands on my head facing the wall, as if everything is all right.

It's Uncle Boris. He sends Paul back to bed, and says: "You can stay facing the wall for another hour. A dickey bird tells me you're the ringleader."

He goes back downstairs and Nathan leans out of his bed by the door and pulls me back into his room. He sits up in bed and smiles. I look up at the ceiling and tremble, wondering what he wants from me. He takes hold of my hand and puts it under his covers; it lands on something warm.

"Now push. Up and down like this." He puts his hand on top of mine and says like this. The thing in my hand begins to get harder and bigger; it reminds me of holding onto Nathan's inner tube while he's fixing a puncture. But when I hit something bristly I know it's not his bicycle inner tube and I flinch.

"Shush."

I try my hardest not to cry out as I push up and down. All of a sudden something wet and sticky spurts onto my hand. Nathan pushes me back out onto the landing and I rub my hands on my nighty, facing the wall as if nothing has happened. But Sparky makes me cry by appearing above my head and pulling at my hair. Uncle Boris can hear my sobs and sends me off to bed.

Every night that week as I go up to bed early, Nathan is waiting for me by his door. He says if I open my mouth he'll spread our secret, beat me up and chop my hands off.

When my punishment is over, Nathan leaves me alone for a few weeks. And then he begins calling me into his room again. I go, as I am scared. Sometimes he pushes my head under the covers and says suck it. Every time he says this, my body goes stiff, and he pushes my mouth on top of his hard thing. But I keep my mouth closed. "Suck it!" I hold my breath and squeeze myself out of my body and fly up onto the ceiling. All I can see is Sparky jumping all over the bed. And then I can feel Nathan pulling at the neck of my nighty. I fall from the ceiling onto the bed and try my hardest not to swallow the bitter taste in my mouth.

He bribes me with sweets, shares all his games with me. I get to play with all the boy toys I've dreamt of: Scale Electric, Sabbuteo, Soldiers and his chopper bike. We become best friends. He even pays me a shilling to take his sheets to the laundry when he wets the bed. I accept; it's worth it because in the mornings I can prove to my school friends it's not me who wets the bed and that I'm just on an errand before school, just like them.

Sparky begins to visit me regularly. When he arrives at mealtimes, and in class at school, he pushes me out of my seat and I have to shout at him to leave me alone. Everyone begins to say I must be going mad as I talk to myself all the time.

Aunty Claire announces at dinnertime that the third sign of madness is hairs growing on the palms of your hands.

"Whatever next," responds Uncle Boris. "Now you've condemned the Germans for making your husband mad. Now you want to blame something for making you mad."

"Don't worry, Boris, the English are the most demented race in the world," says Aunty Morag. The adults all laugh and finish eating their dinner.

I'm so worried about going mad that when Aunty Claire takes me for my first walk outside of the Village I decide to ask her what the first and second signs of madness are. I hold her hand and trot behind her as she takes me up the high street. Cars zoom by, honking their horns.

"Nigger lover," a woman screams out through a car window. Aunty pulls my hand tight and shouts at me. "Say after me, 'Sticks and stones can break my bones, but names will never hurt me'." But they always do, even if I don't know what they mean. They feel like pins pricking my body. However, to please Aunty, I repeat it and pretend her medicine has worked despite all the goggling eyes in the street.

"Aunty Claire, what are the first and second signs of madness?"

"The men in white coats will come to take you away if you ask too many questions."

I panic. She notices and smiles: "The second sign of madness is looking for hairs on the palm of your hands, and the first sign is talking to yourself." I panic again. I wonder if the men in white coats really will snatch me away. I've been searching for hairs on my hands ever since she told me what the third sign of madness was, and everyone at home and school says I talk to myself.

The high street seems friendlier now and we bump into the coloured boy who spat at me when I first came to the Village, walking with his Uncle. He teases me for holding Aunty's hand, so I pull it away and she gets angry with me again. I can't have the pair of Mary Poppins tights she promised me. So I sulk, drag my feet, and look into all the big shop windows.

"Look, Aunty Claire, a children's home for toys."

Aunty ignores me and leaves me staring into the window. And then all of a sudden, I feel my arm being yanked out of its socket. "Come on, Pauline, stop gawping."

A big sign in the shop reads: No Bill Stickers, and Shoplifters will be prosecuted. "Who is Bill Stickers?"

"The man who sticks bills in the window."

Confused by Auntie's answer, I sit on the pavement outside the shop and try to work out how a man called Bill Stickers can be strong enough to lift up shops. As I try to look under the shop, Aunty Claire pulls me to my feet and says: "I really will send you off to live with the men in white coats if you keep up with these antics."

I protest while still looking at the sign: "How can Bill Stickers be a shoplifter?"

Aunty Claire falls about laughing. "Never you mind, shoplifting is nothing you need to worry about right now."

"Wow! Will I be strong enough to lift up a shop one day?" Aunty Claire laughs again, and says come on, you've had enough excitement for more than one day.

The next time I get to walk up the high street is on the first day of the Easter holidays. Aunty Claire and Aunty Morag try to dress all of us in navy shorts, red and white striped T-shirts, and elasticised belts with a big gold snake buckle, so we look smart for our walk to the forest. Pippa refuses, and Heidi follows suit. Everybody else gives in and does what they are told.

As soon as we parade up the high street people stare at me again and start spitting. Coming up to both Aunties, they tell them how disgusting they are. "You're a shame to our race. How could you sleep with a coon?" Some of their children run off screaming Sambo, Abbo, Paki and Yids. A woman with a chin that almost reaches her tummy and smelling of greasy bacon and chips, says to Aunty Claire:

"You dirty whore, look at you with all these children from different men. Blond, ginger, brown, chestnut and a wog. You should be locked up in a workhouse."

Aunty Claire laughs and tells us all to chant Sticks and Stones. But nobody pays attention.

Instead Nathan asks: "Why can't my dad drive us all to the forest in the minibus?"

"Yeah, why do we have to walk?" demands Simon.

Pippa and Heidi ask: "What will we do if we bump into our friends from secondary school?"

The rest of us try to hide behind Aunty Morag's fat body. Both Aunties pretend we're back in the Village and everything is normal. They begin singing "Onward Christian Soldiers", and we all troop behind them up the high street. When a passer-by calls out "Look, there go the Banana kids" Pippa blows a fuse: "That's it. I'm not doing anything associated with Dr Barnardo's again. When I leave, I never want to hear that name again." She storms off in the opposite direction and pretends she doesn't know any of us.

It's the second day of my Easter holidays and I'm sitting on the toilet all on my own. Paul has left the Village to go and live with his real family and Keith is out with his social worker for the day. It's lonely here on my own. I begin to wonder when the Angels will come and take me away as I've decided there is no hope of a real mummy or daddy for me. I keep on pushing and I can't go. I push with all my strength and I still can't go. So I jump up and down on the toilet seat, closing my eyes and clenching my body as tight as I can until my tummy almost splits open. And then I hear a plop. I look and see two brown stones at the bottom of the toilet. I call out to the Aunties and nobody appears. I begin banging the door and screaming, "Aunty, I've been to paper toilet." By the time the cleaner, Mrs Wilson, arrives I am hysterical and she tries to calm me. Finally I can hear what she is saying. Aunty Morag and Aunty Claire have gone shopping for Easter Eggs and all the other children are out playing with their friends.

Mrs Wilson closes the door, and asks me to be quiet. One of those horrible big lumps grows in my throat and Sparky tries to dance in front of my eyes. But I'm not interested in him right now. I just want to go out and play with my other friends. I call out for the Angels, but they can't hear me, so I close my eyes and try to magic Aunty Morag and Aunty Claire to appear. Finally they do and Aunty Morag calls out:

"Minstrel, what are you still doing on the toilet?"

"I'm waiting for you, Aunty."

"You silly bean. You should have pulled the chain and gone out to play."

After that day, I never have to go to paper toilet again. I am a big person now, like everybody else in Cross Cottage.

6

The first time I meet Wunmi she is wrapped up in a brown paper bag, along with white chocolate rainbow drops. A scrap of paper reads: Happy Easter, love Wunmi. She has long brown wavy hair just like my favourite Barbie doll and is the prettiest lady I have ever seen.

"This is from your mother," Aunty Claire says.

"I haven't got a mother, she's dead."

"I don't know what you do, Minstrel, in that tiny head of yours. But it's full of the wildest dreams."

"I think about Sparky and when I'm going to visit the Angels next."

"Exactly. It's time you grew out of that imaginary nonsense."

"It's not imaginary."

"Button it, Minstrel. It's time you had proper friends."

"They are proper friends," I howl.

"And so is your mother. She has written to you all the way from London, and will be visiting you very soon."

"No," I fume and drum my feet all the way upstairs. Sparky is waiting for me under my bed. I tell him we haven't got a mother. "Our mummy died in Bristol when we both left to come and live in the Village." He flickers underneath my bed and I know that he agrees. I share my rainbow drops with Sparky and bury the photo in the brown paper bag under my pillow.

I dream of falling through a jungle. A huge elephant catches me in his trunk and throws me back up into the sky where the Angels live. I fall again towards a man as dark as the night with brilliant white paint all over his body. He is surrounded by gold coins. As I try to look at his face, I can hear the sound of galloping horses and screaming voices. The man disappears in a puff of smoke and just before I hit the ground, covered in writhing snakes, I wake up shouting: "Don't take me!"

The brown paper bag is in tatters. Aunty Claire comes racing into my bedroom: "I did warn you that if you insisted on eating cheese for supper you'd get awful nightmares." She tucks me back up into bed and kisses me on my forehead. Aunty Claire doesn't mention Wunmi for a while, and I forget all about her.

It's Duke's birthday and we can all invite one friend along to his party. I've wanted to show off my new friend Terry to everyone in the Cottage. Her name is Theresa but she likes to be called Terry for short. She lives on the same green, in Bible Cottage with her sister and four boys. She is tall with brown curly hair just like George from Enid Blyton's Famous Five books. She is coffee-coloured, with a squashed nose and big lips. Aunty Morag doesn't like her, she complains about me hanging round with a tomboy, who has a mouth as loud as a foghorn.

Terry is good at sports and even better than some of the boys at football and cricket. Aunty Morag says she is a proper little tomboy, and I better watch out because it's catching, but I don't care. Terry doesn't mind getting her clothes dirty and playing some of the dare-devil games like bordering.

Sometimes eight or more boys and a few girls climb up onto a makeshift wooden platform. One of us has to hand a rope hanging from a tree branch with a large knot at the end up to someone on the platform who is waiting to leap off. The rope swings to and fro with one person on it. Then in turn we all jump onto the rope, sitting on top of the person who has just jumped before us. By the time there are six of us holding onto the rope, it's hardly swinging anywhere near the platform, but we still have to jump. Most girls have chickened out by this time, but not Terry.

She dives for the rope and misses, landing on the ground and breaking her right arm. Once it is out of plaster she is back lunging for the rope again. I secretly wish I could be as brave as her.

Terry likes me because I can beat her at running races and climb trees higher than her. She also thinks I live in the best Cottage because on hot summer days we bring a table and chairs out and eat dinner on the front lawn even though Aunty Morag complains about some of the kids in the Village who kick up a storm in the sandpit just as we are eating our meal. Gossip has spread around the Village that Cross Cottage is posh, so she is excited to come to tea.

The day of the party, I come home from school for dinner – soggy carrots and turnips with liver. I push it around the plate, and drop some in my serviette for Sparky.

"Stop playing with your food, Minstrel," Aunty Morag bellows.

"I'm not, I'm eating," I insist.

"If you don't eat your dinner, you'll get it for your tea." The others at the table laugh and I know it's true because I have watched our Aunties force-feed some of the others with leftover fossilised dinner for tea. So I try my hardest to take a few mouthfuls, but it hurts too much to swallow.

Aunty Morag says: "You're not having dessert until you eat up your dinner." But I don't care; it's tapioca and nobody likes it because it looks like frogspawn. By the time dinner is over, I've made a scarecrow's face on my plate. Aunty Morag sends me back to school, instructing me to tell Terry that she can't come to the party tonight. Terry says she doesn't want to go to a stupid dog's birthday's tea party anyway and stops speaking to me for one whole week.

I come back home from school in a sulk, but hope that Aunty Morag has changed her mind and I can run round to Bible Cottage and tell Terry that she can come for tea after all. Instead I'm ushered into the dining room where everyone has a friend except me. Duke is running around the room barking with a funny Mickey Mouse birthday hat on his head. Duchess is sleeping under the table, so I give her a big kick as it's all her and Duke's fault that everyone is ignoring me. My dinner plate reappears with the same old food, only this time it's been rearranged on the plate in an orderly fashion. I'm sure one of the Aunties has put on more vegetables, but I daren't say anything because Aunty Morag would have my guts for garters. While everyone sings Happy Birthday, my tears pour gravy all over my food. All I can think of is the pudding and Duke's birthday cake. Everyone looks like jelly, ice cream, or chocolate cake and so I just keep on staring at my plate to stop me from crying. Finally Aunty Morag asks me why I'm not eating my food today. She whisks me off to the bathroom, puts her hand on my forehead, tells me to open my mouth wide, and places a cold spoon on my tongue.

"Oh look, you've got tonsillitis. You could have had jelly and ice cream after all. If only I had known earlier."

I give a sigh of relief and think about all the party games taking place in the playroom.

"Go on up to bed."

"Can't I have some chocolate cake?" I plead.

"Definitely not. That will make you cough, and then your tonsils will swell even more."

My face drops to the floor.

"Well, you can't stay down here spreading all your germs to our visitors. Whatever next?"

I go up to bed, stay there for three days. Everything is back to normal when I come back downstairs.

However, Terry still has the hump with me, so I find a new best friend. I meet her one day sitting by the sandpit. She is making daisy chains. I sit down beside her and ask if she likes butter. Her blue lips make a big smile and I pick a buttercup and point it under her chin.

"You do! Look, your chin has gone all yellowish." She takes hold of my wrist and puts the daisy chain she is making around it. And says: "Friends forever."

"Friends forever," I reply. I pick a dandelion and give it to her for a present. She squeals and says: "No, I'll wet the bed."

I giggle. "Don't be daft, I picked the dandelion, so it's me who's supposed to wet the bed. But I never have yet."

So she puts it in her pocket. Her eyes stare like marbles while her blue lips do all the talking. She has hair the colour of honeycomb, and her face reminds me of my old doll Gabriel. She is much smaller than me, with dimples in her cheeks.

"What's your name?" I ask.

"Annabel. And yours?"

"Pauline."

"I live in Souls Cottage over there. Is that your Cottage?"

"Yes."

"How old are you?"

"I'm seven, five months, three weeks, and six days."

"How many hours?"

"Oh… I don't know. How old are you?"

"I'm ten, soon I'll be eleven."

"Do you believe in Angels?"

"Yes I'm going to live with the Angels soon."

"You can't, it's not your turn."

"'Tis."

"Who says?"

"My Aunty Isobel does."

"How comes you don't have to wait your turn?"

"Because I'm going to die soon."

"You're too young to die, silly."

"No I'm not."

"Who says?"

"The doctors."

"I don't want you to die."

"There is nothing else the doctors can do."

"Why?"

"I've got a big hole in my heart."

"What's that?"

"When Jesus made me he forgot to put a valve in my heart."

"Can't they give you stitches?"

"You're the one who's silly. It's not like a big cut."

"Are you scared?"

"No, because I know I'm going to heaven, and all the Angels will look after me there."

"What's heaven like?"

"Aunty Isobel says I'm the luckiest girl in the world, because heaven is the most beautiful place on earth."

"Annabel," her Aunty calls out aloud. "Come on, it's time you were indoors." She hugs me and whispers in my ear, friends forever. I repeat friends forever back, and we both go home to bed.

We play every day after teatime by the sandpit. I teach Annabel how to fly out of her body and make friends with the Angels. I ask the Angels not to let her die, now that she knows who they are. I pray to God to not let Annabel go to heaven. But the Angels don't listen to me, and God forgets to answer my prayers. Two months later, I rush out of my front door after tea to play and Annabel isn't sitting there waiting for me anymore. I know she has left me to go and live with the Angels. I run indoors and hide myself with Sparky under my bed. I wake up the next morning not knowing how I've ended up being tucked up in my bed.

7

"You're to dress in your Sunday best," Aunty Claire says, shaking me awake in the morning. I look at her wide-eyed and remind her it's Tuesday.

"You don't have to go to school. I'm taking you out for the day."

Aunty Claire calls me Pauline today, so I know we're going somewhere special. I choose my favourite summer dress with big red roses on it, a blue sailor's jacket with an anchor embroidered on it and a pair of brown sandals. Aunty Claire even lets me carry one of her red handbags. I am so excited and wonder where I am going. A gigantic black car pulls up outside the back door and beeps its horn.

"Come on, Pauline, the horn is for us, grab your coat." Aunty Claire follows me into the car. There is Aunty Isobel sitting next to the driver, playing hide and seek under a large floppy hat. She hides her face while saying good morning to me. I get into the back with some of her children from Souls Cottage while Aunty Claire sits beside another adult who I don't know. Nobody is talking in the big car and all I can hear is Aunty Isobel sniffing. When the car stops, I pluck up the courage to ask where we are going.

"To church," Aunty Claire says.

"But it's not Sunday."

"Shush, Pauline, our little friend has died and we've come to say goodbye."

I can't see Annabel in the church. And my head is swimming. Annabel and I are supposed to be friends forever. I don't want her to be dead. Then I see a wooden box being put into the earth.

"Annabel," I scream. "You haven't waved goodbye." Aunty Claire pulls me back. "Why isn't she going upstairs to heaven?" Aunty Claire gives me a dig in my ribs, and I know to be quiet.

A man in a white nightdress says a prayer and throws a cross into the hole. I try throwing myself into the hole too but Aunty Claire has me tight in an arm lock. She whispers, say goodbye. I wave to the hole and scrape my feet all the way back to the big black car.

Sylvia, one of Annabel's friends from her Cottage, comes up to me and Aunty Claire lets go of my hand. "Why don't you two become friends," she says and begins to talk with Aunty Isobel.

"Annabel has already gone to heaven. She's not in that wooden box," says Sylvia.

"How do you know?"

"My brother says when you die, they put all your toys and clothes in there so nobody can steal them."

I want to run back and put all the daisies, buttercups and dandelions I can see into the box. But it's too late; we are already driving towards home in the car.

Aunty Claire lets me have the whole afternoon off school. So I change into my play clothes and sit by the sandpit wondering if Annabel is living in heaven with the Angels yet. A ladybird lands on my arm and I let it crawl all over me. Then I catch caterpillars in my hands. I run inside hoping one of the Aunties has a spare jam jar. Aunty Morag leads me into the pantry and points to a shelf full of empty jars. I choose one that has had honey in it and still smells sweet. I run back outside, but the caterpillars have gone.

"Pauline," Aunty Morag calls, "it's dinnertime." I run back in, but stop first to smell the roses in the front garden. Something tickles my nose; I sneeze and out falls a caterpillar.

"Look, Aunty, a caterpillar is in my nose."

She laughs. "You must have brought it in from the garden. Now come on in, it's dinnertime. You can spend all the time you like looking at them this afternoon."

So I wash my hands for dinner. Nathan is home from school because he has a dentist appointment, and Keith, Simon and Inez have the half day off from the Village school too. It is my favourite toad-in-the-hole and suet pudding. The pudding comes out of a steaming white clay pot, with golden syrup dribbling all over it. "Yum yum, bubble gum, stick it up your mother's bum," Nathan whispers in my ear. I giggle and Aunty Morag shouts "Minstrel!" I know now that my holiday is over. And I'm no longer Aunty Morag's or Aunty Claire's pet for the day.

Because I am the youngest I'm always the last to be served dessert. I gobble down my first portion without even tasting it, singeing my tongue so I am the first in the queue for more. When seconds are served I make it as last as long as I can by taking tiny mouthfuls. Aunty leaves the room to get some water, and Keith whispers in my ear with his mouth stuffed with pudding: "My mum says this is what heaven is like. Always in happy land."

"You haven't got a mummy."

"Yes I have."

"No you haven't. Stop telling fibs."

Aunty Morag catches us arguing with each other and tells us both to leave the table. All of a sudden I am sad. I hate having to leave nearly all my seconds and wonder if this is what hell will be like if I am too naughty to go heaven. And then I remember the pantry. I sneak in and take a packet of raw red jelly. I run out of the front door to the sandpit. I open my jelly and before I manage to take a bite, it falls into the sandpit. The sand looks like it has given the jelly an awful rash. I'm so mad that I do a war dance all over it.

And then I remember the caterpillars. I catch one crawling along the grass and put it into the honey jar with rose petals and leaves. I punch holes in the lid with a pair of scissors and hide it under my bed with Sparky. I check the jar everyday, and before long the caterpillar has spun cotton wool so I can't see it anymore. I want to watch it become a butterfly. I use a magnifying glass, and borrow Nathan's telescope, but all I can see is a cocoon. And then one day I look under my bed and see a beautiful yellow butterfly with dark spots. I wait until after teatime, then take the jar outside and sit in the same place where Annabel and I always sat, open the jar and set it free. I can hear Annabel whispering, friends forever; she leaps up like a breeze of warm wind. Her spirit brushes me and we fly together with the Angels. She never takes me to her new home; instead she brings me back, waves goodbye and whispers, friends forever.

I become best friends with a girl in my class called Sally. She has a mummy and daddy who live and work in the village, and everyone thinks she's spoilt because she's not an orphan like the rest of us.

A month after we become friends, Sally's mother dies. Aunty Claire says we are to mark Mrs Ainsworth's death so nobody is allowed out to play after tea. Sally was supposed to be one of the lucky kids with a real mummy and daddy, but now she is half like one of us orphans in the Village. I wonder if her mummy can look after Annabel in heaven. Sally's says her mummy has died of cancer and God has taken her to heaven. And after a year of being sick in bed she is going to rest in peace.

Her parents, who are friends of Aunty Claire and Uncle Boris, live on the memorial green in Psalms Cottage. All their children are moved out into other Cottages when Mrs Ainsworth becomes seriously ill. Sally comes to our Cottage when Mr Ainsworth needs a break. We are in the same class at school, so Aunty Claire says it's my job to keep her happy.

Two days after her mummy dies she comes round to play.

"Minstrel, go upstairs and find a toy for Sally."

"That's where I keep my favourite ones. Why can't I give her one from the toy cupboard?"

"Minstrel, upstairs and none of your lip."

I force myself upstairs with Sally reluctantly following behind. It feels like the times I have to go up to bed and know that Nathan is waiting upstairs in his bedroom to take something away from me. I don't want to give anything away. I pull out a battered teddy from beneath my bed, a broken yoyo, and an old pack of picture cards. "I can't choose, you choose," I mumble.

Sally crawls under my bed and pulls out a brand new dolls' tea set.

"I'll have this," she says with a big smile. For a moment I hate her, and then I notice how happy she is for the rest of the evening while we play.

The next time she comes round it isn't so bad when Aunty Claire tells me to find something to give to Sally. She rushes upstairs and looks under my bed, but this time I get Sparky to scare her by catching her hair on my bed springs. I have hidden my best toys in the playroom downstairs.

8

Our Village church closes down so Aunty Claire says we have to go shopping for a new one. We team up with the Fredericks who live with six children in Holy Cottage on the sports green. Mr and Mrs Fredericks wear big crosses round their necks, which almost knock you out when they kiss you hello on the cheek. They sing when they speak, and Aunty Claire says that's because they're from another country called Scotland.

Uncle Boris stays at home with the dogs and the rest of us pile into the minibus. I end up having to sit next to the coloured boy who spat at me when I first came to live in the Village. His name is Pedro. He has blue-black skin, a big grin and is always getting himself into trouble. We sit together in the new church too. We both hate the service because it goes on forever, and so we begin to talk.

By the next Sunday we are the best of friends. Every fourth Sunday it's church parade, and the service never seems to end. People carry flags and banners up and down the aisle for what seems hours. Pedro asks me if I want to play noughts and crosses. He pulls up his shorts and scratches four white lines on his leg. When the game is over he offers his other leg, and so we forget to close our eyes and pray. Instead we play throughout the service. It makes the time go quickly until one week he gets fed up with rubbing his legs with spit and tells me to pull up my dress and chalk four lines on mine. He digs his nails in me, and I almost yell from pain. But once we start playing I forget the pain and try my best to win.

Aunty Claire says the church is too far away for us to go to Sunday school, and so we have to find another. The Fredericks agree, but us kids are not so pleased as it means we will have to start going to church twice on a Sunday again. Uncle Boris manages to get us out of having to go to the Village church on Sunday evenings by regularly inviting the Fredericks and their children over for pilchard and lemon curd sandwiches. He lays a white lawn in our playroom and we all sit on the sheet and scrap over Mousetrap and Monopoly while the adults sit on big chairs and argue over the prices of a Grandfather Clock, furniture and jewellery as they watch the auction programme *Going For A Song* on television.

Aunty Claire finds a High Church just outside the Village. It's a ten-minute walk through the back gate and into a park opposite the Village. The service is the same every week: we read from a blue book and repeat holy words after the minister. He sings long sermons in Latin, eats the body of Christ and drinks the blood of Christ. And we all get a chance to do the same. We go up one by one and kneel before Jesus Christ on the cross. I get to eat Christ's body, but when it comes to drinking his blood, the minister hammers me on the head and says, May the Lord be with you.

He hits all the children on the head and I wonder how old we have to be to get to drink some blood. Pedro says he's

52

never going to drink the blood when he grows up because he doesn't want to be a vampire. When we go back to our seats, the minister begins singing in Latin again and our eyes are closed for prayers. I feel the wooden handle of the velvet purse being pushed into my hand. It's time to let go of the sixpence I've been clutching. Pedro dares me to take some money out of the purse. But I just quickly put my hand in and drop my sixpence on top of the others. Pedro says I'm a baby and shows off the shillings he's taken from the purse when we walk home.

On most Sundays there is a man who sits at the back of the church on his own. He always wears a grey suit, carries a big black umbrella and has snow-white hair. Pedro nicknames him the wizard. When the congregation begins to say "Our Father, Who art in Heaven, Hallowed be thy name" the wizard begins to shout: "Bang, bang, bang. Der, der, der!" The wizard is pretending to be at war. He is throwing invisible hand grenades and making them explode with his mouth; he stands at ease and then salutes the minister. Then he charges through the pews with his black umbrella swinging as if he is holding a machine gun. Pedro ducks and yells: "Watch out for the wizard!" and Aunty Claire pokes me in the back to tell me to stop staring. After church she explains that the man was shell-shocked in the war. So when he starts making noises we must pretend nothing is happening, as everyone is welcome in the Lord's house.

On Sunday afternoons we're sent off to Sunday school. I'm allowed to go with Pedro, Terry and her sister from Bible Cottage. After a month Pedro discovers a rock 'n' roll disco.

He convinces Terry, her sister and me to go with him. We use our pocket money to get in. The disco is full of children between the ages of seven and eleven who have skived off Sunday school. We learn to do the twist, jive and rock 'n' roll. It's much more fun than Sunday school. But Terry confesses to her Aunty and on the third Sunday, Aunty Claire and Mr Frederick turn up and drag Pedro and me out by our ears. Aunty Claire docks my pocket money and makes Pippa take me on my own to Sunday school. Pippa moans, but she's secretly happy because it leaves her two hours to be with her boyfriend who lives outside of the Village.

I hate Mrs Swift and so does Pedro. Every art class she complains about me spilling the paint and smudging the charcoals all over my paper. When I show her my finished picture, she says: "It's impossible for you to have drawn and coloured it in so nicely. You must have traced it from a book."

"I did draw it, Mrs Swift."

"You'll lose that tongue of yours if you keep on telling white lies."

"I did draw it."

"Stop fibbing, Pauline Charles. Someone must have drawn and coloured it in for you."

"It's not true."

"You are the messiest child in the whole school and your handwriting is atrocious, so how one could ever believe you have drawn that is beyond me."

I sulk and don't try to prove it was me who drew it because I don't want to tell Mrs Swift about Sparky and how he makes me use my left hand. Instead I make my hand dead. I say goodbye to it and pretend it isn't on the end of my arm.

It isn't worth using it anymore because it just gets me into trouble.

Pedro hates Mrs Swift because on his eighth birthday he moves into her class and she catches him making paper aeroplanes and water bombs out of his brand-new exercise book, so she pulls his shorts down in front of the class and gives him the slipper.

We hatch a plan. Every Thursday when we have writing lessons, Mrs Swift puts the letters on the blackboard that she wants the class to copy. She tells us to study them carefully while she leaves the room to fetch fresh ink and quills. As soon as she leaves for our writing tools, Pedro and I walk to the front of the classroom where her handbag is sitting on her desk. Pedro opens the bag and takes some loose change out of her bag. I tell everyone not to tell, otherwise Pedro and his two brothers will beat them up. Nobody answers me; they just stare with fear, and we sit down at our desks as if nothing has happened.

As soon as class finishes, Pedro and I sneak out of the Village to the sweet shop across the road. We buy sherbet lemons, two sherbet dips, two curly wurlys, cough candies, bonbons, rhubarb and custard, jelly beans, and a bottle of All Whites Lemonade. We split everything in half, stuff the sweets in our anoraks, and guzzle down the lemonade before sneaking back into the Village.

I arrive home to find Mr Fredericks and Aunty Claire waiting for me at the back door. Aunty Claire has her arms, legs and eyebrows crossed, while Mr Fredericks is spluttering over a cigarette. As soon as he catches sight of me he throws it to the ground, screwing his tiptoes all over it, takes hold of his crucifix and waves it in my face.

"Where is Pedro?" Mr Fredericks asks.

"He's gone home."

"Really."

"Yes, Mr Fredericks."

"Where is Mrs Swift's money?" Aunty Claire asks.

"In her handbag at school."

"And how do you know that?"

"I don't know, Aunty Claire."

"What's that bulging out of your pockets?"

My tummy does a big forward roll onto my lap. And I feel sick from all the sweets and lemonade I have stuffed down in the past fifteen minutes.

"What's the matter, Minstrel?"

"Nothing. It's not my fault." I hand Aunty Claire one bag of sweets, but she says everything, so I rifle my secret feast out of my pockets and give it all to her.

"Whose fault is it?"

"I don't know, Aunty Claire."

"Upstairs, Minstrel. What does the eighth commandment say? Thou shalt not steal. I think you better write it down a thousand times." Her eyebrows rise into her forehead, she goes all boss-eyed and uncrosses her arms and legs. Then she gives a scary smile. "What do you think, Mr Fredericks?"

"How about a million times?" he says grinning and still waving his crucifix in my face.

"A million times, that's impossible."

"Yes, Minstrel, a million and one times, and you and Pedro are not to play together again. Do you hear me?"

"Yes, Aunty Claire."

I lose all my pocket money, have to wash up the dishes after tea every day and empty the coal bunker every morning. I can't go out to play and have to go to bed early for one whole month. Nathan starts touching me again and the only person I dare tell is Sparky. But he does nothing to help me. Nathan says it's our secret and if anybody finds out about it he'll beat me up. I don't understand why these same words didn't stop someone splitting on me. Pedro and I never find out who told tales, so nobody gets beaten up.

Pedro is sent away to boarding school. Aunty Claire says next time it will be me. So I make paper aeroplanes and water bombs too, but Mrs Swift ignores me. I have to stay in her class and in Cross Cottage. Every weekend Pedro comes back to the Village, and we play out on our bicycles and roller skates where nobody can see us. He teaches me to play splitseys with a penknife, and how to build tree camps and fires. He also shows me how to make extra money by going bottling. We look in dustbins and in backyards for empty bottles, and sneak across to the sweet shop for returns.

Even though I have no pocket money I still eat sweets in secret on Saturdays when everybody else has gone shopping for theirs. I can't wait for the summer holidays when Pedro will be back in the Village for six whole weeks.

9

Aunty Claire says, "I've got a lovely surprise for you. Close your eyes." She takes hold of my hand and leads me down the passage from the kitchen into the special front room. I can tell it's the staff front room because I can smell Uncle Boris's tobacco lingering in the air.

I open my eyes and opposite me is a coloured woman sitting in a chair. She has three identical scratches on each cheek and hair like Shirley Bassey. I let out a scream and try to hide behind Aunty Claire, but she pushes me in front of her and says: "Behave yourself. This is your mother and she's travelled all the way from London to visit you. Now go and show her around the Village."

"She's not my mummy," I shout back. Sparky trips me up on the carpet and I have a tantrum. I pull my slippers off and throw them at Wunmi and I continue to scream: "No, I don't want to." Wunmi doesn't move; she sits with a fixed smile, still as a photograph.

Aunty Claire calls for Uncle Boris, and pulls me onto my feet. "Do as you're told, Pauline." And I know she is serious because she only calls my proper name when she is spoiling me or if she is very cross with me.

Uncle Boris enters the front room and demands to know

what all the fuss is about. I jump up onto his back and shout:

"She's not my mother, take me away."

"Pauline, listen to me, this is your mother and you have to be very polite. She has come a long way to see you."

"I don't want to see her." I kick my legs into Uncle Boris's ribs as if he is a horse, but he doesn't gallop off like we do when we are playing rodeo games.

Instead he puts me down and places his hands on my shoulders and stares into my eyes. I'm scared. I know he is angry because his face is red and he's spitting out words nobody can understand. Whenever Uncle Boris is furious, Aunty Claire says he must be speaking Yiddish and we better keep out of his way.

I count up to ten. I call out aloud for Sparky's help because I know Uncle Boris likes my friend as he always inquires how Sparky is.

"Can I take Sparky?" I ask feebly. The smoke stops pouring out of Uncle Boris's nose and ears, he leans over me and says: " Ya, ya, ya! If you must. Oy vey."

So I try to be on my best behaviour and show Wunmi the Village. I take her to see Dr Barnardo on the memorial green. He is made of black stone and looks down on all the children who play on his seat. I jump up onto his seat and lie underneath him. I put my hand up towards the statue and tell Wunmi: "This is my daddy."

"You don't have a daddy," says Wunmi.

I sit right up in his seat and correct her: "Yes I do. His name is Dr Barnardo and he is very dead."

Wunmi smiles and gives me her hand. I pull my hand away and say, meet Sparky. But Sparky doesn't appear and so she smiles again and asks me if I would like some sweets. "Yes please," I answer and take her across the kinder green towards the shop. Pedro is playing on his bike. His legs are shining like pieces of silver paper today because his mummy has been to visit and rubbed cooking oil all over them. He calls out: "Is that your mummy, Pauline?"

"No, I don't have a mummy. This is Wunmi who's come all the way from London to visit me."

"Wunmi, that's a funny name. Is she an Aborigine?"

"No, I'm African," Wunmi proudly replies.

Pedro rides with no hands, placing his hands under his armpits and making monkey noises as he cycles off. Just before we enter the shop, Wunmi says she has a treat for me before we buy the sweets. She walks me up the high street and takes me into a jewellers shop where she pays a bald-headed man to stab my ears. He sits me down in a big black leather seat, puts his feet on some pedals and up I rise into the sky. I feel like a dalek. Then he pulls a lever on the armrest and my back and neck are pushed into a right angle. He sprays cold steam onto my ears and then stabs them so quickly that I don't even have time to scream. He wriggles gold rings into my ears and says: "Don't worry, they won't be sore for long."

My ears feel like they have grown twice the size and I've lost my appetite for sweets. Wunmi take me into the café next door and I ask for fish and chips. I forget I have rings in my ears until I get home.

When Wunmi says goodbye she says she'll come to see me next week. I wave goodbye to her and hope that means she'll never come back to visit. All the kids in my Cottage laugh at me and say only cows wear rings. So I pull my new earrings out and throw them into the bin.

When next Saturday arrives everyone except Aunty Morag and me go to the forest for the day. She dresses me up in my

Sunday best and says: "Pauline, you must be very polite when Wunmi arrives. I want you to show her how well Uncle Boris, Aunty Claire and I have brought you up." She looks me in the eyes, smiles and bribes me with an extra fifty pennies in my pocket money if I'm a good girl. Then she adds: "As you've got a special visitor, you can sit in our staff room today."

"Can I have the fifty pennies now? I want to buy some sweets."

"Certainly not. First you have to show Wunmi and me what a charming young girl you can be. Now run downstairs, she'll be here soon." The window looks onto the kinder green and I can see almost as far as the old church near the main front gates. I stare through the window and beg Sparky not to let her come. I wish so hard that every time I see someone walking from the direction of the church, my heart leaps. I wave at them, hoping they can see me saying goodbye. An hour has passed and Wunmi hasn't turned up.

"Can I go out to play, Aunty Morag?" I call out.

"I don't want you getting your brand-new tartan pinafore dirty." She enters the front room with a glass of orangeade and a rock bun to eat and says: " Don't worry, there is most probably a problem with the trains." My heart sinks into my shoes but I continue to hope that the train never comes.

I bite into the bun and a burnt raisin makes one of my teeth wobble. It begins to hurt so much that tears come to my eyes and I can't drink or eat any more.

Out the window I can see Pedro and Terry playing splitseys. They're standing opposite each other; he throws a penknife and it sticks into the ground. Then Terry moves one leg to the penknife, pulls it out of the ground and throws it again. This time Pedro stretches his leg to the penknife and throws the knife up into the air. It lands so far away that

Terry topples over and they begin all over again. Some of the older boys are playing bumpseys on the seesaw. Charles from Bible Cottage brings down the seat so hard with his bottom that his friend Scot flies high up into the sky, clapping his hands and screaming. He lands back on the seesaw seat suspended in mid air, and then slams it down so hard that Charles rockets up into the sky, screaming. The children next door are quietly playing jacks with stones on the front lawn. And some boys and girls are playing knock down ginger on the front green. All I want to do is go out and play. Dong dong the clock tower chimes. Wunmi still hasn't arrived and I begin to worry that I've killed her off too.

I hear singing from the backyard, for he's a jolly good driver, and the back door flies open. I can hear everyone running in from today's outing. Aunty Morag says I can leave the front room now and change into my play clothes. Heidi and Inez run upstairs to our bedroom and ask me if I've managed to scare Wunmi away again this weekend. My body stiffens and they seem to understand because there have been times when they have both been dressed up and their relatives haven't turned up. They try to cheer me up by looking under my bed and calling for Sparky, but Sparky is already with me living in my head. I've learnt it's better for him to stay there than under my bed, because nobody can take him away from me.

Heidi and Inez chase me around the bedroom, calling, Sparky, Sparky. We jump onto the chairs and dive under the beds too. "Sparky, Sparky, come on let's all of us play with the Angels," Inez teases. They both grab me and tickle me so hard that it hurts and my tummy almost bursts open. I manage to get away and run straight into one of the legs of my bed, knocking my wobbly tooth out. Aunty Morag crashes up to our bedroom to find out what is all the noise about.

Heidi says: "I was trying to pull out one of Pauline's baby teeth while Inez was trying to hold her still."

Aunty Morag puts me to bed with my baby tooth snug under my pillow and I try to stay awake as I've never managed to catch the tooth fairy who comes to put a sixpence under my pillow. But I fall asleep and dream of Aunty Morag stroking my face and tucking me up tight in my bed like a jam roly-poly.

My teeth begin to grow enormous like elephant tusks. And one by one the ivory tusks fall onto my pillow. The midnight man with the white funny patterns on his body visits me again. He smiles. His teeth are massive too. He gives a huge cough and his teeth turn into gold coins which scatter all over my pillow. I wake up with a new shiny shilling under my pillow, but I'm upset that I've missed the tooth fairy again.

Several more times I'm dressed up in my Sunday best and made to sit in the front room while everyone else goes on an outing on Saturday afternoons. My magic power seems to have worked as Wunmi doesn't turn up.

The summer holidays are here again and I have six whole weeks off school. It's so long that I'm worried about what I will do every day. But my worries disappear on the second day when a huge lorry turns up. Pedro is hollering: "Stop, stop!" and most of the children under eleven who play on the kinder green watch with shock as it empties the sandpit next to the water fountain. Pedro organises all of us in a protest. He tells us to march round the green shouting: "Give us our sand back!" The lorry makes a loud blast with its horn and we all run away. Once it's gone we all march round the green, chanting our demand again. Then Pedro suggests we build a camp in the empty sandpit. It's the best we have ever built and it's for everyone. All the other camps in trees or the orchards, or in the adventure playground, belong to gangs.

We strip wood from some of the derelict Cottages on the memorial green and find carpet to put down on the stone floor. We fix battered corrugated iron on top for the roof and use old doors to partition a section for the girls and a section for the boys. Terry is put in charge of the girls and Pedro of the boys. It's where most of us between six and eleven tend to live this summer whenever we're playing out. We take turns to guard it so the lorry can't come back to empty the other sandpit in front of my cottage, or demolish our camp. All the children who live on the other greens are jealous and their house parents come to have a look. But when the adults decide to let us keep the camp, we all become bored. The girls start arguing with the boys over who should be doing the guarding, and eventually we all fall out.

Next a lorry drives into the Village and pumps all the water out of our swimming pool. Pedro dares Terry and me to come swimming with him with our clothes on. We rush off to the pool on the memorial green, but the wooden gates are closed, so we climb over the walls. That's when we discover the empty pool.

We climb back over and run back to the kinder green screaming "Help, help, someone stole our swimming pool." We bump into Uncle Boris and the dogs and he falls about laughing. He pulls a funny face and says; "Yes, our swimming pool is closed forever."

I pound my fists on his tummy and say: "No, we want our water back."

"Yes, give us our water back," both Pedro and Terry echo. Uncle Boris throws a stick for the dogs and then looks down at us and tells us not to worry because we're soon going on holiday where there will be lots of water to play in. Pedro's Uncle, Mr Fredericks, comes running up and says: "What are these three up to now? Pedro, get back to the cottage, you and Pauline are not supposed to be together."

"Uncle, the swimming pool…"

"Oh, the swimming pool, what's all the fuss about, we can visit another swimming pool at the Garden City, the neighbouring children's home down the road."

"Hooray," all three of us shout, and run off in the opposite direction so that none of us have to go home for the rest of the day.

The next day two minibuses are stuffed with us Village kids. We're off to the Garden City children's home for a swim. When we arrive, boys and girls are waiting for us at the iron front gates, their hands crammed with mud bombs which go splat on the minibus windows. When we park, one of the Uncles gets out first and asks the children to welcome their neighbours from the Village. They scream that they're the true Dr Barnardo kids and then run off laughing. But they are waiting for us outside their swimming pool.

Pedro shouts out "Wankers!" and a war begins. Mud bombs are exchanged between us until the staff from their children's home hoses all of us down with ice-cold water. The City kids run off and we enter their swimming pool.

"The Vill kids rule ok," some of the older kids chant, and they jump in off the diving boards fully clothed. But we can still hear the kids from the City outside shouting "Out! Out! We want you out!" Our Aunties and Uncles tell us to ignore their taunts and enjoy our swim. When we leave the pool, our minibuses have "City Home Rules OK" scribbled all over them and some of the windows are broken. But there are no children in sight.

Pedro pokes his head through a broken window and

shouts: "Keep your green slime and snails to yourselves! We're used to a clean swimming pool."

"Yeah, keep your green slime and snails," we all repeat after him. Just then, a mud bomb lands on Pedro's right cheek. But it doesn't stop us from coming to use their pool again. But each time we have a mud bomb fight before they let us swim.

10

I've saved three pounds from my pocket money to take away on our holiday with me. We're off to Broadstairs again: it's Aunty Claire's favourite place. Our minibus is packed so high that nobody can see out of the windows. Duke and Duchess are squashed under the seats and the rest of us are piled on top of bedding and cardboard boxes. Inez and Keith are travel sick all over me, Nathan wets himself because he can't hold on, and Heidi, Pippa and Simon all argue with each other. Every fifteen minutes, Aunty Claire or Aunty Morag tells us to be quiet while Uncle Boris knocks all the pots and pans onto our laps every time he turns a corner.

It seems to take forever to get there, and most of us are exhausted. But once we arrive our enthusiasm returns and we unload the minibus in half an hour. The church hall is our new home for two whole weeks.

The mattresses are turning green and there are creepy crawlies living in our blankets and pillows, stored from last year. We spend the first day airing and disinfecting everything that was left behind.

When it's sunny we go down to the beach and stay there all day, making sand castles with moats and underground tunnels. We run into huge waves and collect crabs that have been washed up by the sea.

When it rains Nathan takes me to the amusement arcades. It's one of my favourite places – money clinking, bells ringing, pistols shooting and trumpets playing silly tunes. Reds, yellows and blues flash all over the arcade, and I can see Sparky flashing too and having so much fun. I put a penny in the slot and let Sparky pull the arm while I gleefully wait for three plums, three melons, or one cherry and a bar to stop spinning and freeze in front of my face. Nathan groans and says I'll be cemented there all day waiting for very little profit. He insists on teaching me all the tricks of the trade.

He shows me how to fold a piece of gold or silver paper from a cigarette packet and squeeze it through a money slot, blowing it onto the moving mat of the "wheel 'em in" machine. When the piece of paper lands on the lines, the money comes spitting out from the top of the machine. If it falls between the lines a loud bell rings and we have to run for our lives. Nathan shows me how to knock the moving steps covered all over with money so it comes whooshing out. And he gives me a handful of foreign coins to use in the penny machines. So my three pounds savings are doubled to six in a day.

On rainy days we always eat our meals in the church hall. So when Nathan and I get home with our secret windfall, Uncle Boris wants to know where we've been all day as everybody has been looking for us. Heidi is mad with me because she wanted me to fray the bottom of her jeans for the church disco tonight. Her jeans are far too long so she has to wear huge platform sandals to make the jeans fit. Before she can grab me I run off to the toilets to wash my hands for dinner while Nathan tells a lie about losing our way home. Once everybody is seated around the table, Aunty

Claire says grace. Then, because it's our holiday we don't have to wait to be spoken to.

"What's for dinner, Aunty Morag?" I ask

"Potato and rabbit stew."

"But you said Tufty had to stay at home!" I wail.

Inez butts in and says: "If we eat this we'll all get mitsamotosis and die."

Nathan announces: "The Lord has asked me and Pauline to become vegetables today and so we got stuck in the mud on the way home. That's why we're late home for dinner tonight."

"Stop this rubbish and shut up and eat," says Aunty Morag. Every one else ignores our pleas and seems to be happily enjoying their dinner. None of us three eats our dinner and we're lucky we're on holiday because Aunty doesn't save it for tomorrow's dinner.

Aunty Morag says I have to help her do the washing up. As soon as I enter the kitchen I blurt out, "Nathan says you killed Tufty and tomorrow we'll be eating him in our steak and kidney pies."

"Tufty is alive and well and the cleaner, Mrs Wilson, will look after him properly."

"Whose rabbit did you cook then?"

"You've got nothing to worry about. It's alright to eat this rabbit as he doesn't belong to anybody."

"He must have a home, Aunty Morag."

"Somebody found him in a field and took him to the butchers so somebody kind like us would buy him." Before I can say anything else, she gives me a shilling and says: "Run along to the sea front and buy chips for Nathan, Inez and yourself." We stuff ourselves with chips. The next day all of us forget we only eat vegetables and tuck into steak and kidney pie with mash.

I hate Sundays. Whether it is hot or not we still have to go to church even though we are on holiday. I beg Uncle Boris to take me with him when he takes Duke and Duchess out for a long walk on Sunday morning. But he says this is his holiday too and he doesn't want to be pestered by children every day. Besides, the local congregation would be very upset if I didn't turn up.

On the first Sunday that we are there, we all sit in one pew like one big happy family. The vicar announces: "We are very happy to welcome the visitors from Dr Barnardos. We are also very fortunate today as some of the Barnardos children are going to come up to the front and sing us a little song."

Sparky rocks me back and forth. My heart begins to jump out of my body and I become all sticky. I can feel Nathan and Inez pushing me out of my seat. Keith pinches me and says: "If I have to go up to the front of the church, you do too." Only four of us manage to make it to the front; Pippa, Heidi and Simon refuse to go up and hang their heads in shame. I'm sardined between Nathan and Inez, who keep me propped up. I can feel Sparky trying to push me over from behind and I am beginning to feel faint. I look down at my feet and I am hoping the floor will open and swallow me up, or all the people in the church will disappear. But nothing happens. When I look up a tidal wave of faces is coming towards me, and I feel like I'm standing out at the front all on my own.

The church organ begins to play a hymn. I should know the tune, but all the words have fallen out of my head. Keith punctures his lungs while Nathan and Inez stamp on my feet either side of me, and I wake up and stand to attention. I can see Aunty Claire and Aunty Morag mouthing the words, "I know that Jesus loves me, Jesus loves me". I join in with the others, singing louder and louder until I can't feel my feet on the ground anymore. It feels good until Inez kicks me in the ankle and tells me to shush. I shut my mouth abruptly and become aware of all the people in the church who are clapping for me. We can all go and sit back down now. But Sparky and me don't want to go. He flickers in front of my face and jumps all over my head, and tries to spin me round.

He begins to sway me to and fro and I enjoy the giddy feeling, but Nathan drags me back to my seat. "That's the last time I make a fool of myself up there," Inez spits out. "I'm not seven or eight anymore. I'm nine and very grown-up." Both Aunties ignore her, and say: "Well done. You all did Dr Barnardos proud."

The next morning Nathan has got back at me for making a fool of everyone at the front of the church. I wake up to crabs crawling over my pillows and scream the church hall down.

Our two weeks are over and it's time to go home. Aunty Morag and Aunty Claire shout at everyone until we're all in the minibus sandwiched between grubby buckets, spades, bedding and clothes. Only this time we can see out of the windows on the way home.

I don't want to go back to the Village as Pippa has grown up and is leaving to go and live in a hostel, Keith is going to live with his granddad, and Heidi has sworn on her life that she is leaving next. But I have no choice; our holiday is over and Uncle Boris is driving us home. When we get back a new boy moves in. His name is Warren and he is seven years old. I decide not to like him because he's seven months and two days younger than me. I'm no longer the baby of the house and it's not fair. He gets all the attention and is spoilt rotten.

He has brown hair and freckles all over his body, and everyone wants to play join the dots on his face. He stamps on daddy long legs and, if they can still crawl, he tears the legs off to see if they can still walk. He wants to play kiss chase with me, but I spit in his face.

I don't want to play with him. I want my friends back who are still on holiday. Pedro's Cottage is in the Isle of Wight, and Terry's household has gone on a climbing holiday to Mount Snowdon. And I have three more weeks of my summer holidays left.

11

Overnight it seems that some of the boys in the Village have changed. Us girls can't beat them in fights anymore. All of a sudden they're much stronger and start talking about the thing in between their legs. Some of them climb up trees, take out their willies, and see how far they can pee while they sing "My Dingaling".

Everyone is scared of a boy call Cecil; he's sixteen and lives outside the Village. His mates say that he is as thick as two planks, he's gone barmy and that at night the birds come and nest in his Mohican hairdo. And that's why he didn't get to join the local Hells Angel gang. He is a friend of four brothers who all live in Trinity Cottage on the sports green. We call them the Teddy brothers because they wear winkle pickers, drain pipes and all have jet-black quiffs.

Cecil brings a moped into the Village and teaches the Teddy brothers to do wheelies on their chopper bikes as well as on his moped. He shows them how to kick down doors and karate chop through bricks and piles of plates, and bite off dead chickens heads. If they don't do what he says, he brings his two brothers into the Village and beats them all up. If he asks a girl to go out with him, she can't say no, otherwise she'll be scarred for life.

So when a message came that Cecil was looking for me, I knew I was next. There was nothing I could do except find out what he wanted. I knew he didn't want to ask me out as I was almost eight, but he might want me to climb through a small window to help do a burglary. One of the Teddy brothers instructs me to cycle over to the hospital and wait by the morgue for Cecil. I cycle over at great speed, but as I get closer to the morgue I begin to wobble. I remember some of the boys bragging about who they have laid behind the morgue. I don't know what they mean, but some of the girls they brag about have changed. They stop smiling and laughing, even playing outside for a while and you know that something is wrong. I stop just before reaching the morgue as Aunty Claire has always said: "Never walk past the morgue because you never know who may jump on you. And God knows who will follow you back home."

I wait. I stare at the morgue, and for the first time, Sparky doesn't look like my sparklers or flashing lights anymore. He is a five-year-old boy with bright pink skin and a mop of thick black hair sitting on the roof of the morgue. I can feel him trying to tug me onto the roof, but I'm scared. I know I have to sit here and wait for Cecil, otherwise he may damage me for life. Some boys he had beaten up needed crutches and he had made some of their faces look like the red-hot sun. Sparky is happily chatting away to his friends on the rooftop, and I can hear strange shrill voices in the wind. A child and three adults with missing arms and legs sitting on the grass in front of the morgue beckon me to join them. But the fear of Cecil's arrival keeps me perched on my bicycle seat. I hear the sound of another bike. I wobble like one of the jelly fish that I had caught in my bucket last week at the seaside.

He stops. "I've been looking for you."

I had been looking out for him too. But I'm not going to tell him that. Instead I keep on wobbling on my bike. Sparky calls my name and, just as I try to put my feet on the pedals to join him on the roof, I'm on the ground and Cecil is on top of me with my skirt pulled up and knickers pulled down. Something hard and wet is trying to ram its way between my thighs. I squeeze my legs so tight that my whole body goes numb, and I can't feel anything anymore.

He leaves me on the grass beside my bike, gobs in my face and calls me a frigid whore. I don't understand what he means, but manage to wave goodbye. He cycles off. Sparky calls out to me and asks me if I want to go home with him. But just as I find the strength to say yes, a butterfly lands on my forehead and I can hear Annabel whispering, it's not your time yet. I leave my body on the grass and float towards the morgue. Flashing lights blind my sight and I can only hear Sparky's urgent voice. "Bye bye, Pauline. I've found my friends now."

"I'm your friend, Sparky."

Annabel whispers to me, I'm your friend too, and sucks me back into my body.

I leave Sparky on the roof of the morgue and cycle back home. I brush my teeth and sit down to tea with everyone else.

"What's wrong, Pauline?" And I freeze. Why is Aunty Claire calling me Pauline? Is she cross with me? Was she there at the morgue? Has somebody followed me home? I slump into my bangers and mash and wake up with a very cold heart. The doctor has a stethoscope on my chest and he is asking me to take deep breaths. But my breath stops at the point it touches my nostrils. I won't let it enter my body. He dissolves a tablet in a glass of water and makes me swallow. As soon as it goes down my throat, I'm chucking it back up all over the bed. The doctor tells me to go back to sleep and he will come to see me tomorrow. Annabel is hovering above my head. I try to reach out to catch her hands. "You can't live with me yet, Pauline, you have to stay here at home." I am too weak to leave my body and follow her, and I am scared that because my body is soiled God won't let me into heaven.

The next day my body is covered in spots from head to toe, and everyone in my Cottage is worried because I've stopped talking. The doctor rushes me to the hospital and just as we drive by the morgue I pass out. I wake up with a nurse dressed in a blue and white apron tick-tocking away at the end of the bed. Her clock is almost as big as her face as it swings from her breast pocket.

"Pauline, you have to start eating, otherwise you will die. It's been three days without food, Pauline. If you don't eat today, I'll have to drip feed you."

I roll back under my sheets, and re-enter my world of dreams. I'm six and a half years old and Uncle Boris is teaching me to ride a bike. He sits me on the saddle, takes my stabilisers off, gives me a big push and hollers at me to hold on. I hold on really tight and pedal as fast as I can, but after five seconds I go whack on the ground and half my body is numb. "Get back on," he screams. I clamber back on, trying my hardest not to cry, and whack bang whollop, I'm off my bike again.

Aunty Claire shouts from the front door: "Boris, you'll make that child black and blue. If you're not careful, she'll end up as black as coal."

Uncle Boris doesn't put me back on my bike; instead he whispers in my ear: "You've got to be brave, Pauline, you can't give up now, I'll give you another lesson next week."

By the time next Saturday arrives I've forgotten about all my bruises and try again. This time it doesn't hurt so much when I fall, and I'm determined to ride my bike. Uncle Boris gives me a big push and I go wheeee all along the kinder green, I hold on so tight that I can't turn the handlebars, so I smash into a tree. I can hear the same shrill voices in the wind as when I was waiting for Cecil by the morgue. The voices are screaming "payback" and calling out my name.

I wake up in my hospital bed to the tick-tock of the nurse's clock. The same blue and white nurse is telling me I must eat, otherwise I will die.

I meet Bobby in the hospital. He is ten years old and loves climbing the walls. He has one leg and a grin that covers his whole face. He is very rude and gets me into trouble, making me throw food against the wall, and telling the nurses they have big noses and smell. He twitches so much that my appetite comes back after a week. I'm eating sweets, cakes, and all my dinners too. The nurses complain to my house parents that I am uncontrollable and most definitely well. But I still have spots all over my body.

The doctor sends me home and says I can't start back at school until all my spots have disappeared. I'm put in a room on my own and made to live upstairs. And Bobby has followed me home. Nathan visits me and Bobby throws pillows and shoes at him every time he comes into the room. Nathan says he isn't speaking to me anymore because there is a rumour going around the Village that I'm a slag. But I don't care, I don't want to talk to him either and I want to be left alone.

Warren comes to visit me in my new room. "Give me a kiss," he insists.

"No."

"Why not? I know all the boys have had you. Show me how you do it."

Bobby and I turn into a rage. I'm bigger than Warren, so

I pull his shorts down and push him to the ground. He holds on to his pants while I yo-yo up and down on top of him and say: "This I how you do it. Just like this. Up and down."

Bobby pulls me off and Warren pulls his shorts up and flees out of the room. He never teases me again and the next time he comes to visit he is armed with a pack of playing cards called "Happy Families".

12

Terry and her gang are running riot up and down the school stairwell. There is so much commotion that nobody is interested by my late arrival into the autumn term. Some of the fourth-year kids are barricading the entrance to my classroom with a banner brandishing the words "Save our School" while other boys and girls are chalking the stairs with "Barnardo's School Rules OK". Terry and her gang are singing "We shall not be moved". A letter has been sent home to our house parents to say that the Village school will be closing down at Christmas due to lack of funds and staff shortages, and that all the children will have to attend junior school outside of the Village.

I join in the riot, while the teachers run around not knowing quite what to do. The headmaster closes the school for the day and we are all let loose to run riot in our adventure playground, swinging on car tyres, and sliding down trees. Some of our house parents come over to the playground to check on us. They are angry too and tell us that they will be sending a petition to the head of Barnardo's in the hope of saving our school.

Some of us kids are overjoyed because we've been told recently that we're not clever enough to take the 11 plus and go to Grammar School. And so we have to stay at the Village school until it's time for Secondary Modern.

When Aunty Claire realises the Village school is definitely closing down and that I get to go to a new Junior school next year which does the 11 plus, she says it's a waste of money because my brain is like a sieve, but I may as well sit at a desk and attempt to do the 11 plus if they're offering it on a plate. Mrs Swift agrees with her, but says to me: "It's unlikely in two and half years that you'll be clever enough to read the exam paper, let alone fill it in. You must learn to count in decimals, Pauline, instead of living in cuckoo land."

Inez is the clever clogs of the Cottage. Because the Village school does not do the exam, she's moved out of the fourth year to a nearby local school so that she can sit the 11 plus. She passes and everybody is singing her praises. I am jealous of Inez because she gets glasses for reading. She has beautiful creamy pale skin, long blonde wavy hair and doesn't have to wear braces on her teeth anymore. And now everyone is calling her a brain box at home. She gets to marry God in a white dress at confirmation classes and is allowed to take Holy Communion. And she belongs to Girls Life Brigade but I can't join because some of the Village kids have given Dr Barnardo's a bad name. Aunty Claire tells everyone that because Inez is such a good girl she's taking her to the Lake District with Uncle Boris and their son Nathan when they next go on holiday. And she might even adopt her.

I'm desperate to be the same as Inez so I steal some of Aunty Claire's face powder and pat it all over my face. But Aunty Morag says that I look so ugly now that I couldn't even be a golliwog on the Robinson jam jar. Next I get Bobby to help me pretend I can't see. Aunty Morag sends me to the opticians to have my eyes tested. Bobby jumps in front of the letters so I can only see the big A and a few other letters. In a week I'm wearing a pair of glasses every hour of the day. They hurt my eyes and make all my friends laugh at me. Inez teases me and calls me Doctor Spock, and I get her back by announcing at dinnertime: "Aunty, Inez doesn't believe you'll ever adopt her and says you're telling lies."

Everyone's face turns to stone and I drop my cutlery onto the floor. Nobody talks, not even when they're spoken to, and we all finish our dinner as quick as we can. Inez ambushes me in the boot room, hitting me with everybody's shoes and wellies, but with Bobby's help I'm stronger now and avoid being really beaten up.

She's moved into Pippa's old room, and Heidi has gone to live with a foster family, so I'm left in a four-bedroom room all on my own. A month later the Jeffreys arrive. Latisha is dark brown like me and moves into my room. Her older brother, Osmond, is half caste, six foot tall and aged thirteen. He moves into Simon and Warren's bedroom. He is a big bully and everyone, including the Aunties, is scared of him. Latisha is in my class, so we become good friends. We keep each other up whispering all through the night. Sometimes we chatter so much that I fall asleep in class the next day. She knows about Bobby and my Angel friend Annabel, and tries to stay awake to meet them.

"Are you asleep?" asks Latisha.

"Yes."

"No you're not."

I sit up in my bed and say: "If you know I'm not asleep, why are you asking me then?"

"Because I was checking."

"When am I going to meet Bobby and Annabel?"

"Not now. I want to sleep."

"Right, that's it. I'm not going to tell you my secret."

"What secret? I thought you had no secrets."

Bobby starts a pillow fight. He drags me out of bed and I take all the pillows from the spare beds. We pummel Latisha, who is hiding under her covers. Annabel is hovering above, inviting Latisha to fly. But she is too busy playing hide and seek in her bed to get a chance to meet my two friends. Suddenly Latisha sits up in bed and scares everyone away, snarling: "I don't have to tell you everything."

"Yes, you do."

"Why?"

"I don't like your brother."

"Snap! Neither do I."

"Why?"

"Because I don't. You started this, you tell me why?"

"He makes me touch his willy."

"Really? I thought he only did that to me."

I throw a pillow from my bed and say: "You're wrong. He's been touching me since you moved in."

Latisha chucks the pillow back and replies: "Is that all? He's been touching me for years."

"What do you mean?"

"Sometimes we have to go and visit our uncle, and he puts us asleep in the same bed. And he says you're the patient and I'm the doctor. And he opens my legs and sticks things in me and makes me play with his willy. And when I wake up in the morning, he says it's a nightmare and I mustn't tell anyone just in case it comes true."

"What about your uncle?"

"What about him?"

"Can't you tell him?"

"You must be mad, Osmond would kill me," and Latisha slips back under her covers.

I can hear crackling in her bed. I jump out of my bed and

pull back her covers. She's eating a packet of biscuits she's stolen from the pantry. I insist on three, one for me and the other two for my friends. She doesn't believe me, but manages to begrudgingly give me all three. I run back to my bed and munch on a Garibaldi biscuit, spitting out the raisins and chanting, "I hate raisins and I hate Osmond too." Then I plead, "What can we do?"

"There's nothing we can do, we just have to do what we're told and pretend it's a dream."

"What about your secret? I'm awake now."

"I've forgotten it."

"Oh, please tell me. Please."

"Promise you won't tell anybody? Shush, I think that's one of the Aunties coming upstairs."

"No it's not, it's the dog. I promise, Latisha. I cross my heart, and hope to die."

"Oh, alright then. There's a secret place I go to."

"Where?"

"Near the bushes by the old spooky linen house. And guess what? I met three gnomes who live in a tunnel under the bushes."

"I thought only ghosts live there?"

"It's my secret. And I'm telling you in those bushes live three gnomes."

"What do they look like?"

"Like how gnomes should do. Stop interrupting me."

"What games do you play with the garden gnomes then?"

"They're proper gnomes, not like the ones in our front garden. I visit their parents' home, which is a tunnel under humps in the ground covered by green moss. And they give me lots of presents."

"I don't believe you."

"It's true."

"Prove it. Take me there."

"No."

"Why?"

"Because you don't believe me. And you have to believe me to see them."

"I do, Latisha, I do believe you."

"No you don't."

"Well, I don't if you won't show me."

"See, I told you so."

"Shush, there's definitely somebody walking up the stairs now."

Our bedroom door opens and Osmond pokes his head in. Both of us shoot under our blankets and pretend we are fast asleep. The door clicks shut. But neither of us dares to talk anymore. I fall asleep thinking of Latisha's world of gnomes, wondering whether I should believe her or not. The next day I decide to follow her, but she catches me before she even leaves the backyard. I beg her to take me, but she just runs off, and says catch me if you can. I decide she's made everything up and just wants to make me jealous.

Latisha has her ninth birthday on Guy Fawkes day and very soon after "I'm Dreaming of a White Christmas" is blasted out all over the Cottage. Nat King Cole moves into Cross Cottage at the beginning of every November and everyone forgets I have a birthday before Christmas. Aunty Claire tells me to stop complaining because I always get one big present for Christmas to make up for how little fuss is made over my birthday at the end of November.

Last year Santa brought me a brand-new three-gear bicycle for my birthday and Christmas, but I still got upset when I only received cards and sweets on my actual birthday.

But I often forget my birthday too because there is always so much happening in November and December. Aunty Morag plays Harry Secombe and George Formby on the gramophone while baking Christmas cakes. This year it's a Hansel and Gretel cake covered with smarties, jelly beans and liquorice allsorts. But we never get to eat it because the whole Village is ushered into the front room to witness what a clever cake-maker Aunty Morag is. And so it lives on the mantelpiece in our living room. Us kids have all had a dig at the sweets, marzipan and icing that faces the living room wall.

Uncle Boris makes punch and leaves it in a crystal bowl in the dining room. Bobby and I often tiptoe in before bed and take sips from the bowl with a teaspoon. It's so yummy and sweet that we sometimes drink a dessert spoonful, but this makes my head dizzy and my legs turn to lead. Sometimes I bump into the other kids sneaking in for a bedtime drink. Uncle Boris wonders how his punch has evaporated in such cold weather. Aunty Claire says: "What do you expect if you offer a taste to every adult who walks through the front door?"

We're often invited to the premieres of West End children's shows in London, and we also get to go to Christmas parties up and down the country. Sometimes they're on farms in big barns, other times, they're held by the Royal Mint, or by wealthy factory owners. Often there are Dr Barnardo kids from all the homes in England at one big party. There are always tons of presents and food and we stuff ourselves silly and play party games all day. Fights break out occasionally between the different homes because we argue over who is living in the best home.

On the coaches back home, we scoff from our goody bags and Bobby and I eat so much that I end up being sick.

Everyone is so excitable and we always sing on the coach journey home.

> "Down in Barnardo's far far away.
> Where we get kicked about ten times a day.
> Egg and bacon we don't see.
> We get sawdust in our tea.
> Down in Barnardo's far far away.
> Early in the morning the Aunties come and shout.
> Get out of bed you lazy sods before we kick you out.
> Down in Barnardo's far far away."

13

I'm nine years old and I still want to believe in Father Christmas because he gives me great presents and answers most of the letters I put up our chimney. Everyone in our Cottage gives presents to everybody, including Duke and Duchess, the cats, our dolls and action men. The presents start piling up around the tree in mid-November, and by December 24th the Christmas tree fairy is living on a hill and all our presents have started flashing. There are so many presents that my eyes hardly ever live in my head. Bobby and I creep downstairs at night and play with all the presents, picking them up and feeling them and trying to work out what they are. When I leave the living room, Nathan, Warren and Latisha are all waiting in a queue. By Christmas Day we've all worked out which presents belong to us.

I love Midnight Mass because the priest smells of perfumes and all the Angels are out to play. Yellow and white Angels fly above my head and in between my legs. They hover round the organ and make a ten-year-old choirboy sing "Once In Royal David City" at a very high pitch. Annabel is flying too and happily playing with her new friends. I'm envious and want to join in and fly, but Bobby has borrowed my body so he can enjoy church too. I can't move. I pretend

I am playing musical statues with the Angels above my head. All I can do is watch the church fill up with the three wise men, the shepherds and visitors from the local town. I get to see Joseph and Mary, the donkey and baby Jesus all living in a stable.

"Aunty Claire, why was Jesus Christ born in a barn on a bundle of hay, if he is so famous?"

She says: "Rags to riches, just like Oliver Twist."

All the children are happy at church and all the adults are sad. Tears roll down their cheeks while they sing "Away In A Manger" and "Silent Night".

When we get back home, Uncle Boris is fast asleep in an armchair, and Aunty Claire and Aunty Morag collapse in chairs beside him and send us to bed although we plead to stay up and open our presents. We go up to bed in a bad mood, but in seconds we're all fast asleep. We wake up to a stocking full of tangerines, dried fruits, nuts in shells, and lots of sweets. Hanging beside it is a pillowcase stuffed to the brim with new dolls, board games, playdo clay, paints, crayons, French knitting sets, bath salts and soaps. Latisha and I run into everyone else's room to see what they have got. Nathan is the only one who is still in his room. He suggests we all go and wake his mum and dad up. When we run into Uncle Boris and Aunty Claire's room, we get a big shock. We see two beds. Nathan says it's a secret, his mum and dad don't love each other anymore.

Latisha says, "Of course they love each other, they've just grown too big for one bed. Let's go downstairs."

We race downstairs to find our house parents sitting in exactly the same place we'd left them in a few hours before, with the rest of the kids demanding to open their presents. Uncle Boris says: "All pressies opened after church."

"No!" We all scream in unison. He roars with laughter

and says: "Okay, you all win. No church today, let's open pressies." He grabs the first one and calls out Nathan's name. All our eyes are glued to his present. Nathan snatches it, tears it open, slings a pair of boxing gloves to the ground and waits for his next present.

Uncle Boris hypnotises us all. He reaches for the next present and calls out Duke. Duke chews open a big rubber bone. He takes another present with Aunty Claire's name on it. She makes us wait by peeling off all the sellotape without tearing the wrapping paper to reveal a new pair of slippers.

Next he calls Latisha's name, and I panic. I am sure Santa has ordered that my presents go back up the chimney because I was sent home from school last week for being rude. Finally Uncle calls out my name. I snatch the present from him, open it, notice a pair of roller skates and drop them to the floor as I hungrily wait for the next.

After two hours all the presents have been opened, and I don't even know what Santa has brought me. Latisha picks up a pair of ballet shoes.

"They're mine!" I scream, pulling at the ribbons. Aunty Morag asks, "Whose are these?" She is holding up another pair of ballet shoes and we both say mine. By dinnertime, I've had two crying fits and a fight. Nathan tries to steal my new record player, so Bobby kicks him between his legs and I yell out: "Spoilt brat. Just because they're your parents, doesn't mean you get all the best things at Christmas."

Then Bobby pushes me over; he is angry that there are no presents for him. The only thing he wants is a brand-new leg. He died in a car crash, and when they cut him out, the ambulance men left one of his legs behind. I tell Bobby that if he goes to heaven he can have everything he wants. Annabel brushes my side with her warm breath, and whispers: "Bobby can't go to heaven. He doesn't want to be dead."

Bobby is inside my tummy grunting, twitching and shaking so much that Aunty Morag thinks I'm shivering because I've still got my pyjamas on. By pinching my skin I let Bobby know that I am happy he is alive and that he is my friend. He quickly calms down and leaves my body alone.

Dinner starts at two and finishes at six in the evening. When Uncle Boris sharpens the carving knife on the back doorstep, we all know it's time to help finish laying the table, with one extra place for someone who may need a meal.

The table is laid with every single piece of cutlery from the dining room drawers. Framing each place mat are two dessert spoons, two teaspoons, two forks, two knives, two Christmas crackers and a coaster. Between all five courses of soup, salad, turkey, Christmas pudding and mince pies, the adults pause to tell jokes and give us kids lateral-thinking exercises to do. Aunty Claire's favourite joke is: "How did the bus get up the hill without a single person in it?" It takes more than a minute to work this one out and none of us can move on to the second course until we get it. Finally she has to put us out of our misery as Aunty Morag says: "Claire, for crying out loud, the turkey will run all the way back to its farm if you don't tell us the answer soon."

Aunty Claire bursts out laughing and says: "They were all married." Aunty Morag and Uncle Boris let out a huge groan, but most of us kids are still trying to work it out.

Uncle Boris claps his hand and says: "This is one for the kids. A carrot, five stones, a hat and a scarf are in a field. How did they get there?"

"Someone put them there, of course," replies Nathan.

"Nein."

"Someone has thrown them out for Dr Barnardo's to collect," I say.

"Nein."

Latisha says: "They've been there all the time."

"Nein."

Aunty Morag gets impatient: "This is impossible, the roast potatoes have burnt and Boris hasn't even carved the turkey yet. You've made me spoil the Christmas dinner again this year."

Everyone ignores her as we try to work it out. Uncle Boris lets all of us ask him yes or no questions, but none of us can figure it out. Then Aunty Claire whispers in my ear:

"It's a snowman."

"A snowman!" I cry out aloud.

"That's not fair, Minstrel. I saw my mum tell you," Nathan shouts back.

"Enough is enough. It's time for the third course," Aunty Morag says before Nathan and I have a chance to get into a fight. Everyone pulls crackers and changes hats for the big feast.

By six o'clock some of us are snoring and some of us are so full that we have to roll off our chairs onto the floor. Bobby and I play roly poly all the way to the living room and then I lie on the floor, rubbing my tummy and listening to Christmas carols on television.

We go through the same epic dinner ritual on New Year's Eve, dressed in our Sunday best. This time we sing many more songs at the table and Uncle Boris lets us kids have a glass of Advocaat and a taste of his Schnapps punch. When Aunty Claire spots an old man with a walking stick passing our window, she runs out to wish him Happy New Year and invites him in to eat with us. He looks like a scarecrow, smells like a toilet and when he opens his mouth, all his teeth fall out. His breath smells like one of the bottles from Uncle Boris's drinks cabinet.

Aunty Claire sits him between her and me. I am so scared that Bobby pushes me onto Latisha's seat. She falls to the ground and Aunty Claire swipes me around the head. The old man smells so much that I am full up before the second course comes round. Because it is New Year's Eve Uncle Boris tells Aunty Claire to stop nagging me. "If she wants to play under the table with the dogs, let her."

So Bobby and I slide off my chair and tie everybody's shoelaces together. Aunty Claire and Aunty Morag are ready to spit fire when they discover what I've done, but, Uncle Boris says: "We should all sit joined at the hip like this and wait until the next New Year arrives, it would make life much easier. Let's all hold hands and sing 'For Old Lang Syne' again."

14

I've waited two whole weeks to get back to school. And now the Christmas holidays are over I'm frightened. The Village school has closed down and we have to walk ten minutes through the park, past my church and down a big long road to our new school. We all walk in single file, wearing grey flannel tunics or shorts, grey blazers and berets, with two Uncles in front and two Aunties behind. Ten of us have been selected for St Matthew's School. When we arrive at the school gates, the children in the playground stop playing to stare and point at us.

"Look, there are the Banana kids," someone yells.

"We're Dr Barnardo's kids!" Terry yells back.

"Do you eat bananas?" another boy shouts.

"No, we eat sandwiches, crisps and sweets," Terry replies.

"Why do you look like monkeys then?"

The Aunties and Uncles tell the children to leave us alone, and the group splits into two halves, leaving Terry, Latisha and me standing on our own. I call out to Warren and the rest of our friends. But they turn away and pretend they're not with us. I wonder what's wrong, why they're pretending not to be our friends. Terry continues to answer back, while Latisha tries to hide her face. The boys who have been teasing us come and circle us, pulling at our hair and trying to touch our skin.

One of them jumps away and screams: "They really are monkeys, look at their hands!"

Another boy says: "They're not monkeys, they just don't wash properly."

"Rubber lips," another calls out.

Terry growls, "I've got Dunlop lips, and you better beware of my tread."

When the bell rings, they all scatter and the adults who have been looking after us say: "Sorry. Don't worry, they'll soon forget you're different and you'll all be playing together as if you're all the same."

"No, we're not. Those three are coloured and people call them names," says Warren.

"Are we really different?" asks Latisha.

"Of course not. We're all the same," Terry protests.

"Exactly. That's what my Aunty Claire says too."

Terry and six of the others are led off to the third-year corridor while Latisha, Warren, and me are led to the second-year corridor. I'm taken to a classroom on my own and as soon as the door opens everyone laughs. A tall teacher with long black hair picks up a cane and cracks it on the blackboard. Everyone is silent and she welcomes me, telling them that they must all be very nice to me because I am an orphan from the local Dr Barnardo's home. Pennies are thrown at my feet but I stand still, not daring to pick any of them up.

On the first day of assembly all ten of us are made to stand up and introduce ourselves and say where we live to the whole school. The hall is cold and windy, and we all shiver through our whole speech. As we file back out to our classrooms I hear someone whisper: "Poor things, Dr

Bananas doesn't give them enough clothes to wear," and the corridor fills with laughter.

At break time, everyone in my class queues at the door of the tuck shop. A stocky boy called Barnabas, with spots and blonde wavy hair, comes up to me and says: "Wogga matter? Are you all white? Nigger mind, go black home and eat your coon flakes and you'll be all white in the morning." Everyone laughs. Bobby begins to jump around in my body, my arms begin to jerk in the direction of Barnabas's head, but his girlfriend jumps in between us and so my fist hits her head and she falls to the ground. The whole class circles around the three of us and begins to chant: "Fight, fight, fight." Barnabas picks up his girlfriend and pushes his way out of the crowd. My new teacher, Mrs Davies, says I should be careful with what I do with my hands.

After my first day nobody ever calls me a name to my face and Barnabas and I become best of friends. We are dinner monitors together, lead debate classes together and play sports together.

Mrs Davies is Welsh, so she teaches all of us to say "Bora da" and how to sing her national anthem in Welsh. She is very nice. She smiles a lot and tells stories about children from all over the world. She even reads stories to us about fairies and gnomes, and I want to start trying my best in class.

Every Monday morning everyone pays their dinner money for the week. And each week Mrs Davies says: "I know about you, Jack, don't worry."

"Miss, why do you always say I know about you, Jack?"

"Haven't you got some work to do, Pauline?"

Barnabas kicks me under the desk, and says: "Jack is poor like you, idiot. He has free dinners every week."

I was confused. I thought only children who lived in

homes were poor and definitely not if you had a mum or dad.

Mrs Davies says I must start behaving myself as I am very clever. She says I'm going to be a famous pianist or chess player. I've never been told this before and begin to walk around on my tiptoes, with my nose in the air. I'm so proud that I want to get rid of Bobby because he's the one who gets me into trouble and makes me take all the money from the younger children who play penny up the wall. But Bobby wags my tail, reminding me that he is very clever too. I am the only girl in the school chess team and Bobby is the one who helps me to win all my games. He sits inside my body and tells me what my opponent is thinking and what moves to make next.

I join the school orchestra. My headmaster, Mr Rawlins, is the conductor. He punches the air and waves his fists as if he's at a football match, and counts one, two, three, over and over again. I play the tenor recorder, and sometimes percussion with Bobby, and we shake everything that rattles.

It's the Easter holidays and Aunty Morag and Aunty Claire pin aprons to their skirts and wear rubber gloves for one whole month. It's the annual spring clean and Mrs Wilson needs help. Everything us kids haven't played with for a year is put into a sack and sent away. This year Aunty Claire and Aunty Morag pull up all the carpets and pull out all the cupboards in the Cottage. I get to polish all the cutlery, shine all the glassware and dust all the plastic flowers.

One day Aunty Claire says: "The Queen is coming to visit the Village and I'm sure the head of Dr Barnardo's will choose our Cottage for the Queen to come and have tea."

So to be sure the Cottage is kept immaculate, for a whole month we eat lunch out on the front lawn, whether it's sunshine, wind or passing showers. Finally the head comes to do an inspection of our Cottage. All of us kids are sent out to play while Aunty Claire gives her a guided tour of our home.

The next day the letter arrives. Our Cottage has not been selected for the Queen; it's Saviours Cottage where Terry is staying while her house parents are away on holiday. She is so excited and says she'll try to smuggle me in. But when the royal visitor arrives, there is an army of flashing cameramen running all around her. Aunty Claire takes me out onto the kinder green to watch along with every other household. "Oh, it's not the Queen, it's Princess Margaret; if it had been the Queen, our Cottage would have been definitely picked," Aunty Claire declares.

I don't really care. I don't like the Princess because she only gives you a hand to shake, and we have to give her lots of presents and throw bouquets of flowers at her feet.

When the television entertainer Jimmy Savile comes to visit the Village, he picks me up, gives me a hug and a bag of sweets. He promises to take me onto his television show if I can think of what I want him to fix. I tell Aunty Claire that I want him to give me a brand-new ten-speed racer, a pair of tap dancing shoes, enough money so I can buy sweets every day of my life, and a best friend who never goes missing.

"That's far too greedy, you'll have to wait until you're bigger when you learn how to choose just one thing," says Aunty Claire.

"I don't want to wait until I grow up. Why can't I have everything I want now?"

"Your greediness and impatience will get you into trouble one of these days, young lady."

I don't ever get to be on *Jim'll Fix It*, and Aunty Claire says: "Don't sulk, there's many nicer things that could happen."

Wunmi

15

I love Giles Brown and so does everyone else. He arrives at St Matthew's School on a skateboard after the summer holidays. He is in the third year like me, and moves next door into Mr Grimsby's classroom. He has sandy-coloured hair that rustles on his shoulders. He wears faded denim jeans with the bottoms frayed just like Heidi used to wear them. He crosses the number seven every time he writes it in his exercise book. We stare at each other in the corridor and every morning we sit opposite each other in Mr Gregory's special English class in preparation for our 11 plus. He slips me smiley notes underneath our desks and I scratch "Pauline 4 Giles" on top of his desk.

I start crossing my seven's too, even though Mrs Davies says she can't understand where I've got the awful habit of writing down a continental seven. She asks me if I don't get bored being different all the time. But I'm not being different. I am trying very hard to be like Giles Brown. He makes my heart jump up and down every time he tic-tacs on his skateboard along the pavement to school. I am part of a long queue of girls who stand in awe of him as he passes us by, and shows off with a slalom in the middle of the road, pivots and then brakes in front of me.

My school friends let out such a huge gasp that I can hardly stand still. And I have to cross my legs because I can feel myself peeing in my knickers.

"Are you an orphan?" Giles demands

"Yes, well no, oh kind of. What about you?"

"Me! I have two mums and two dads and I live with my gran."

"Liar. It's impossible to have two lots of parents."

"No it isn't," he replies angrily.

And then he does a big jump on his skateboard and swivels in the air, landing with his back to me and skates past the line of girls and through the school gates. My friends let out another gasp, almost knocking me down as they run after him. Giles doesn't speak to me much after that. Barnabas says he is angry with me.

"You shouldn't have embarrassed him in front of all those girls. And Giles says you're jealous of him because he has two mums and two dads."

I'm not jealous, I just want Giles to play with me and show me how to skateboard and do wheelies on his flash chopper bike. I'm far too shy to go to school for a while because he stops looking at me in the corridor and refuses to sit opposite me in Mr Gregory's class, and all the girls giggle at me. I make Bobby invent an illness for me. I develop a terrible nosebleed and Bobby pushes me over so that I graze my elbows and arms. Aunty Morag keeps me off school for a week. By the time I am better I have learnt to ride a skateboard and I don't want Giles Brown as my boyfriend anymore.

Lots of children in the Village are being sent home to their parents, if their social workers can find them. One day they don't come out to play anymore on the kinder green and you know they have gone. And then a month or two later they're back on the kinder green causing all sorts of trouble, picking fights with everyone and being rude to their Aunties and Uncles.

Those of us who aren't so unlucky are given Social Aunts and Uncles in place of the dreaded parents. They come to visit and take you out for the day twice a month. And if you're lucky they take you on flash holidays to Europe and buy you presents like a new bike, a luminous Timex watch or a Polaroid camera.

I knew my turn had come when I saw a man and woman sitting cross-legged in Aunty Claire's front room. Aunty Claire calls me in, and they smile sweetly and ask me my name. I hover at the doorway, admiring their gold jewellery and colourful clothes. Mr Drake has a big belly and Mrs Drake is as skinny as a rake. Just as I decide to turn and walk the other way Aunty Claire says: "Go and show Mr and Mrs Drake around the Village, Pauline."

"Do I have to?"

"Yes!"

I give up without a fight and show them my home.

"Are you scared of ghosts?"

"Yes, we are," says Mr Drake and pulls a funny face. So I take them to the linen house, then over to the morgue and try and spook them out. Instead of being scared, they ask me a whole army of questions.

I tell them: "I don't like vegetables. I like being called Pauline. I hate semolina, I want to be an aeroplane pilot. My favourite game is football and I…"

"How about going to see a football match?" Mr Drake asks.

"Wow, can I? When?"

"Chelsea will be playing at Stamford Bridge in two weeks."

"But I support Man United. Can't I go and see them instead?"

"You get to meet all the team and a signed football to prove it," says Mr Drake

"Really? When can I go?"

My first trip out with the Drakes is to meet the Chelsea football team. Mr Drake's father is a director. I come back to the Village in full Chelsea blue strip and everyone is jealous of me. Nathan and Osmond nick my football and play squash against the garage doors. I have dreams of becoming a famous footballer. But these dreams are stopped short.

Out of the blue, Wunmi turns up at Cross Cottage, demanding to see me. She makes a big scene because the last time she came my hair was in two big bunches and now it's cropped like a boy and there are no earrings in my ears. She threatens to post me back to Africa and my two Aunties get scared. She stays for one hour and promises to come back next week.

She arrives the next Saturday at 2pm on the dot, sits me down between her knees and pushes my head into her thighs. She digs a comb into my head and carves railway tracks into my scalp, rubbing it with cool jelly that eases the pain. I try and grab the comb, but Wunmi sends it crashing down on my knuckles and says: "It's bad luck, that's where all your African ancestors live."

After two hours I have a pineapple on my head. All the braids meet up at the centre of my crown. My eyes are in my forehead, and my forehead feels as if it has married my scalp. I am to scared to smile just in case my scalp splits open and spills blood everywhere. Wunmi promises to come back in two weeks times. I keep on looking in the mirror to see where these ancestors live, but Bobby says don't bother, I have him and Annabel to play with.

I ask Aunty Claire if I can sit in her room the next time Wunmi is due to arrive. I wait by the window and ask Bobby to help me make her not come. She's five minutes late and I think my magic power is working again. Then I catch sight of a coloured woman walking towards me across the kinder green. I throw the chairs around and Uncle Boris comes running in. He picks me up in a fireman's embrace, slings me over his shoulder and takes me upstairs to my room. Aunty Claire is sitting on my bed, waiting for me. "I know you don't like Wunmi, but you are going to have to learn to. Social Services have given her a flat in London on the condition she starts to come and visit you. And today she's going to take you away over night."

Aunty Claire packs a carrier bag with my favourite Beano and Bunty annuals, a toothbrush and my nighty. I sulk all the way to the station. It's my first time on a train. I peer through the window and watch the colours turn from green to grey. I wave goodbye to the ponies and to the dead bodies in a graveyard, then I'm sucked into a long dark tunnel. I close my eyes and hold my ears, but Bobby's voice is ringing out; he doesn't want to travel to London and refuses to play with me. When I am not so scared, I look at the long red line I have to travel on, and start playing a game. I imagine it is a Monopoly board where I get to land on every stop. But when we join a blue line all the way to Pimlico I know I am not home playing with all my friends. We come upstairs for air and there are big red double decker buses lined up everywhere. I stop and stare at all the coloured people who pass me by with their polished brown skin and neat balls of hair.

There isn't any grass where Wunmi lives, just a little flowerbed in the middle of the courtyard. Some girls are playing two balls up against a wall and boys are riding around on roller skates. I run to join in with the girls but Wunmi pulls me back and says: "I don't want you playing with those English children; you've been brainwashed enough."

I sulk again and scrape my shoes along the ground. We enter a dark damp building. An old man sits in the corner with a bottle of whisky in his hand. "Top of the mornin' to you all. Jeezus, Maree, and holee water for me sins. Won't you give a poor sinna some money this mornin'?"

"It's the afternoon, not morning," I chuckle.

Wunmi orders, "Just walk."

I pretend not to see him, but Bobby trips me up and I fall into the old man's lap.

"Jeezuz Maree, Muvva of Chrise, what do we have here?"

Wunmi pulls me up by the scruff of my neck and says: "Keep on walking."

I stride up the stairs two at a time and, after one hundred and twenty-six giant steps, I am on the top floor standing outside her door. She unlocks her flat and pushes me in.

"This is your room," she points.

I've only had a room to myself when I've been sick so I am thrilled. It's shaped like a shoebox with a bed that takes up nearly all the room, and a wardrobe jammed up at the end of it. But there is room enough to make camps underneath the bedsprings. I jump up and down on my bed, hoping to entice Annabel or Bobby to come and play with me. But before I can bring them into my new room, Wunmi is telling me to behave myself before I crash through the floor. She says goodbye and leaves me on my own for the rest of the day. I read my two annual books three times each before she comes back at night.

I wait for her to call me out of my room. When she does she is plucking a chicken for tomorrow's lunch.

"I'm bored," I announce.

"Who do you play with in the Village?" she asks.

"Annabel, Bobby."

"Bobby?"

"Yes, and Terry, Pedro, Warren and…"

"How dare you play with boys!" The carving knife flies out of her hand. Bobby pushes me out of the way, and it hits the wall and falls to the ground.

"I'm taking you home now, you ungrateful child."

"Good," pops out of my mouth. Wunmi gets onto the phone and screams down the mouthpiece. When she slams down the phone she says: "Your Mr and Mrs Steinburg are leaving soon. What will you do then?"

"It's a lie. They're not leaving. They're my house parents, not you."

She says nothing more. I am sent to bed and in the early hours of the morning she packs my plastic bag, travels with me on the train and dumps me at the Village gates. I run as fast as I can back to Cross Cottage. But it's not the same house I left behind yesterday. Everybody is bad-tempered and nobody is happy to see me.

Aunty Claire and Aunty Morag call me into their staff room, and I prepare myself for a big telling off. They sit me down and say: "We are leaving the Village, Pauline." I stare through the staff room window onto the kinder green and I wonder why people always leave.

"Aunty Claire, I want to leave the Village too."

"You can, you can go and live with your mother."

"No. I want to go and live with Annabel in heaven. Or join Bobby in his world."

"Haven't you let go of all that hocus pocus yet?" asks Aunty Claire exasperatedly.

"It's not hocus pocus. We all know you talk to the Ouija board when we go upstairs to bed. At dinner last week you even said the Spirits had warned you that you were going to fall down the stairs."

"You shouldn't be listening to adults talk."

I jump up and bounce my feet like a pogo stick. Bobby is pulling my body up and down, and I say: "No! No! I won't let you leave." I run out the front door and jump into the sandpit and kick up a big sand storm with Nathan, Warren, and Latisha. Inez, Simon and Osmond are sulking in their rooms upstairs. None of us know what to do with the news.

Latisha says: "It must be true. Uncle Boris and Aunty Claire don't love each other anymore."

"What about Aunty Morag?" I ask.

"She's just a copycat," says Latisha.

Nathan says: "No she's not. My mum and dad are leaving because they only love me."

Warren punches him in the mouth and a big fight breaks out. Latisha and I run out of the sandpit and call out for help.

16

Everyone is sulking. It's the first day back at school after the summer holidays. Nathan, Aunty Claire, Aunty Morag, Uncle Boris, Duke and Duchess leave behind us kids, the cats, rabbit and hamsters, and drive off in a van. They wave and promise to write to us from the Lake District, but none of us believe them, and we all argue and fight for a week over who we think was the favourite.

When we stop arguing, we all become excited because the Village can't find us new house parents. This means we move into the holiday home, Saviours Cottage, six doors down. Everyone wants to live with the Blooms, as they make homemade bread and cakes. I'd been wishing for almost a year that our house parents would go on holiday so we'd get to live in their Cottage for two weeks and pig out on all the homemade treats everyone has been gossiping about. Uncle Boris used to say: "Those poor kinder, they move in as lean as a bean, and tumble out looking like German sausages. Best you stay with Aunty Morag when we go on holiday." We complained, but Aunty Morag would make us pancakes every night to keep us quiet when they went away.

Mr and Mrs Bloom are old, have grey hair and wear glasses. Uncle George pulls the curtains every morning, singing: "God bless you, my children, it's time to get up." At breakfast we say grace before we eat and then end with a Bible reading. We're allowed to talk at the table and ask him questions.

"Uncle George, why did you come to work in the Village?" I ask one day at teatime.

"I had a message from God. One day he appeared at my bakery and said, 'Go be one of my servants and tend to the work of the Lord. Go forth and tread firmly on the path of God.'"

"What did the message say?" I ask again, trying to conceal my laughter. Inez is digging a fork into my ribs, so I do my best to be polite and let out a loud sneeze.

"That I should leave everything behind and go look after the children of God."

"The only message I care about is moving out of the Lord's house very fast," says Inez.

"Never fear, my dear. It is safe here in God's house."

She tuts and Aunty Julie tells her to leave the table. I believe Uncle George. When he puts us all to bed, he recites sermons to himself on the landing, and the only route Osmond can take to bed is from the playroom to his bedroom. So Latisha and I can get to sleep in peace every night.

At breakfast the next day, Uncle George opens his Bible, looks directly at Inez and reads: "Remove the board out of your own eye before you remove the speck out of others."

Inez rages and disappears for twenty-four hours. Bobby is very quiet in God's house and the Blooms think I am a good girl. We get to live there for Halloween, my birthday, Christmas and the New Year.

Our first set of new house parents come to tea to meet us. Inez announces she doesn't believe in God, Warren and

Osmond pass wind all the way through our meal, Simon doesn't turn up, Latisha refuses to speak to them, and Bobby and I throw food all around the room. They leave in disgust. Uncle George and Aunty Julie read a sermon from the Bible, ending with "Love thy enemy like thy neighbour" and send us all early to bed.

A new girl from Saints Cottage moves in as her Cottage has closed down too. Her name is Penelope. She is fourteen, wears a long black ponytail, and all the boys in the village fancy her. Inez and Penelope become best friends. Her Aunty had left quite suddenly and so all the kids in her cottage have been scattered around the Village. Penelope doesn't talk very much, but when our next house parents arrive, she organises a campaign. Before the Witters visit us, Uncle George threatens us with burning in hell. So we are all on our best behaviour when they arrive for tea.

The Witters move into our old home, Cross Cottage, but none of us want to move back there. So Penelope and Inez write hate mail and post it through the door. They also get the boys to shove dog pooh through the letterbox. Latisha and I tie string to the letterbox and bang it very loudly. When Mr or Mrs Witter answers the door, we cut the string and hide behind the conker tree. The Blooms say we can't live in Saviours Cottage anymore because we have upset the Lord. Uncle George insists that we all have to repent and ask the Witters for their forgiveness.

The Witters have three children who they hide until we move in. Sheila is the eldest at eleven, and Cindy and Adrian are eight and six. Bobby and I pull their hair, Latisha spits in their faces, Warren swears at them all day long and nicks their toys, Inez and Penelope stay out late at night and Simon and Osmond pretend they don't exist.

"It's not you Dr Barnardo's kids who need looking after,

it's our own kids," says Mrs Witter as she locks herself in the staff room and rings for the big boss. After two months of us fighting with their children and being rude to our new house parents, they leave. We get to move back into Saviours Cottage for six whole weeks and stuff ourselves with food again. Penelope, Inez and Simon say they're not moving anywhere; they are old enough to look after themselves. So an Aunty moves into Cross Cottage, cooks their meals and sleeps over at night.

Our next house parents are called Mr and Mrs Maddox. They've heard all about us, and so bribe us with big chocolate Easter eggs. Uncle Perry walks as if he has just been thrown off a horse and has a snout which looks like the pigs on the local farm. Aunty Faith scurries around like a mouse and is very quiet. And she tries her hardest not to tell us off. They are Born Again Christians and take us to big parks to hear people preach. They take us to see Billy Graham in a massive tent city.

The Blooms had converted me in Saviours Cottage by encouraging me to read the Bible every night before I went to sleep. So when we arrive at the tent city, I want to listen to the Lord's word. But Latisha and Warren irritate me because all they keep on doing is taking the mickey out of the preacher. Latisha says "Repent and you shall be saved" and Warren throws his anorak over my head. He whacks me on my back and says: "Can you hear the Lord knocking on your door? All you have to do is unzip the zipper and let him in." He lifts the anorak and whispers loudly: "Boo!"

"Shush, have you got ants in your pants?" a lady with a baby says behind us. So I move into the next row of chairs on my own.

After five minutes away from my friends, I begin to feel the Lord knocking on my heart. My heart starts beating so fast that I'm not sure when to let the Lord in. I feel so excited. My head is very light and I can hardly stand. I listen some more, and the next thing Annabel is pulling me out of my seat. I am going up to be saved. I want to ask Billy Graham to wash away all my sins, so I can repent and follow the Lord. I want to ask him if he can scrub my body clean of Cecil, Nathan and Osmond, so I can marry and go to heaven. But he doesn't ask me why I've come to see him. He doesn't even talk to me. Instead he throws water in my face and says: "Go forth. You are now a lamb of God."

I stand rigid. My heart is pounding fast again. I wait for a badge or certificate to say I have been saved. But a fat lady with a pram is pushing me out. I still stand rigid, not wanting to budge, and wonder if this is the moment I get to go to heaven. But Annabel lures me out of the tent with her soft warm breath. The cool air wakes me up and I can see Uncle Perry and Aunty Faith waiting to congratulate me. They tell me I have to be good now, as this is what God expects.

I last for one whole week and then I begin to protest about having to go to church in cold windy parks. And I help Inez and Penelope to barricade themselves in their room when the next Born Again Christian convention comes around.

17

My magic powers seem not to be working anymore. I've stopped dreaming of the painted man and all his gold and ivory piling up under my bed. Bobby has been quite calm in my body and I can't seem to make Wunmi stay away from the Village for very long. Sometimes she turns up and other days Bobby and I manage to keep her away. The Drakes have stopped taking me away for weekends without saying why. And I realise my turn has finally come. It's my time to leave the Village. I plead with my house parents, and they say there is nothing they can do. I even tell them that Wunmi has hit me with a wooden spoon, but they say it's better I stay in England than be sent home to Nigeria. Annabel won't visit me at the moment because I keep on asking her to take me to heaven, and I ask Bobby to make me do something that will stop me from having to go and live with Wunmi in London.

Uncle Perry and Aunty Faith say not to worry, that I can stay to do my 11 plus and if I pass I can even go on holiday for the last time with all the Cottage. The big exam day finally comes. We have assembly in the big windy hall, then return to our classroom and sit down for ten warm-up questions. The bell rings and we can all go out for ten minutes. Eighteen kids go mad playing aeroplanes, motorbikes, and racing cars, all with high-pitched sound affects. When the bell goes again, I am so exhausted that I almost forget the importance of today. This exam is supposed to change my life, says Aunty Faith.

"If you pass you'll go to a grammar school and have the opportunity of a lifetime, the chance of going to university. Your mother will be very proud of you."

I sit back down at my desk, look at my questions, and tears spatter down my cheeks as I can only think about the day when I have to leave the Village.

Bobby flashes in front of me. "I don't want to go and live with Wunmi, so what can I do?" Bobby advises me not to answer any of the questions because if I fail Wunmi will not want a dunce to look after.

I read the questions; they're almost identical to the ones we've had in special English every morning for the past two years. But I can't think of an answer for any of them. I don't even feel well enough to guess between possible A, B or C answers. Instead I try to count how many floorboards there are in the exam room.

"Half time," Mrs Davies calls out.

As I look up at her she winks, and I remember her telling me I have to pass! It will be the making of me. I look around and all my friends are busily writing. I pick up my pen and hurtle through the questions as if I am in the dodgems at the fun fair.

The bell rings just as I get to the last question. I tick any box and pray to God that I have passed.

I forget about the exam and make the most of my summer holidays. We go to Bournemouth and stay in a church hall. We're too grown up for Sunday school, and Aunty Faith and

Uncle Perry can't find one of their Born Again Christian gatherings, so we really are on holiday. Simon, Inez, Osmond and Penelope disappear every day; they say they don't want to be shown up by us youngsters. So the rest of us pretend to all the local children we meet that we are rich kids and hang out in the arcades all day long doing dodgy things. I teach everyone to poke a coat hanger down the machines so all the money comes tumbling out. Warren almost gets us caught by trying to exchange a monopoly note for a real note at the change booth. We record the Village national anthem in the record-making booth.

> *"We hate Dr Barnardo's and we hate the Village.*
> *We hate all the staff including the Big Boss.*
> *We don't care really and we don't care what.*
> *We are the Village boot boys!"*

Walking back from the arcades with Latisha and Warren, I spot a silver car with a huge lion on the bonnet. We surround the car and peer through the windows. The seats are all decked out in red leather with matching leather cushions. A burly man with a big beard walks up to the car, and says: "Excuse me kids. Please can I get into my car?"

"Hi, Dad, where have you been all these years?" I cheekily ask.

The man looks down at the three of us and smiles, "Where do you all hail from?"

"We live in a Village in Essex," says Latisha.

"And our parents are very wealthy," I add.

"Is that so? And which village may that be?"

We all laugh. Latisha says: "Well, our father is very wealthy."

"And famous," I chip in.

"You all have the same father?"

"Oh yes," we all chime.

"We're all Dr Barnardo's – ouch, that hurt!" I yell at Warren.

"Blabber mouth," Warren fumes.

"Dr Barnardo, I've heard of him. He's fairy godfather to all the poor little orphans." And then he chuckles, looks at his gold watch and says: "How about I drive you poor orphans home? I better do Mr Barnardo proud."

"Yes, please," we all say together.

So in we all hop into his huge silver wagon, waving our hands out of the window to everybody we pass. We call him Dad and he asks us lots of questions. We direct him back to our church hall and offer him tea with sour milk in a plastic mug. He leaves his address and invites us all to his family home.

When he leaves, Uncle Perry and Aunty Faith are the angriest we've ever seen; they tell us that we should never speak to strange people and definitely not take a ride in their car. We plead for three days for them to take us to visit our new friend and on the fourth day they give in and chuck all three of us in the minibus for a quiet life.

Dad's house has a tennis court, a swimming pool and rolling lawns, and it's like we're back in a tiny version of our Village.

Uncle Perry and Aunty Faith let us stay for the day. We play hide and seek in the grounds with his daughter. Dad says I'm very cheeky and his daughter would love to have someone the same age as me to play with. He says, "You'll get on like a house on fire, she has imaginary friends too."

"My friends aren't imaginary. They're real, just like everyone else."

"Okay, have it your way, but wouldn't you like to come and live with us?"

"Yes please! Will I be rich like you?"

"If you behave yourself."

"I'll be on my best behaviour, promise."

I jump up and down with joy. "Meet Bobby. He's over the moon, and wants to come too." Bobby jumps inside me so much that I puke everything up I've eaten that day. Uncle Perry says; "Enough is enough, we're off," and drags Latisha, Warren and me back home.

By the time our holiday is over, everyone is resentful of me because Dad wants to adopt me and no one else. I am flying as high as a kite. But when I arrive home, the wind is taken out of my sails. It's made very clear to me that the decision has been made to send me back to Wunmi. I have passed my 11 plus and Wunmi is very proud.

Two days later, the time comes. It is a warm September day; the leaves have turned brown, yellow and red, and the prickly skins of the conkers are split wide open, ready to be shelled. Everyone is out to play when Wunmi turns up.

Uncle Perry and Aunty Faith squeeze me tight and give me a book with photos of all my friends. Pedro comes to call for me; he winks and pushes a blue note into my hand, then carries my suitcase across the kinder green. I have a haversack on my back and Wunmi is stumbling behind with books and toys that Bobby has managed to throw out of my haversack onto the grass. I pass the church and stop in front of the closed door. I cross myself just as Aunty Claire did whenever she was worried. I pray for the Father, the Son and the Holy Spirit to save me.

"Please God don't let me leave the Village," I whisper at the church door.

Bobby will not move beyond the church. He digs my

heels into the ground. I fall forward onto the loose gravel and when I look up, I can see Bobby waving goodbye. He turns away, and I know he has run off to find a new friend. I feel Annabel's warm breath. She whispers to me: "Just remember to pray."

Then I remember the Blooms saying: "Pauline, Jesus Christ died on the cross for you, so you could be saved." I know now that all I have to help me at Wunmi's house is the Lord's Prayer.

But I can't pick myself up. I can't even cry. I am waiting for God to save me. However, he is still sleeping in his house.

"Come on. You'll miss your train," Pedro calls out.

I look up and see Wunmi and Pedro waiting for me at the black iron gates.

I force myself to stand up and take another step forwards. Pedro drops my case. I know this is the end. He punches me in the arm and says, just be very brave, and waves goodbye. I hold on to my tears. When they are wrung dry, I have arrived at Wunmi's flat.

18

I am falling through the jungle again. Only this time there is ivory and gold falling from the sky. As I dive head first through the trees I try to catch all of it, but the gold and ivory keeps on slipping through my hands. The painted man appears in front of me, looking just like a big fat African chief. He laughs all over me. Beneath me I hear screaming voices and the sound of cracking whips. Just before a whip licks me, I wake up in my new home, shouting for Dr Barnardo to come and take me home.

I realise there are no Pedro, Terry, Inez, Warren or Latisha in my life anymore. They are all dead. Wunmi kills them off by tearing up all my photographs this first morning when I wake up. I've lost my family. I don't know who I am anymore. Pictures of me beginning life at four and a half are in a pile on the ground. I try to stick them together in my head, but Annabel tells me to try and forget. I remember Uncle Perry saying: "It's for the best, Pauline. You're one of the lucky ones who get to go home and live in a normal family."

Before I can reach down to save a picture of Uncle Boris, Wunmi is shouting in my ear: "I'll teach you to be an obedient African child," and throws everything out which smells of Dr Barnardo's. I shut myself in the toilet and pray for God to take me away. I'm sure he won't let me suffer, so I pray very hard. As I pull the chain, Annabel taps me on my shoulder and says: "I did ask, Pauline. I'm really sorry, God says you can't come and live with me because heaven is full up with too many small children. But keep on praying and God will answer your prayers."

"Please let me come now," I whisper back.

Wunmi pushes the door open and I try to act normal.

"How dare you take so long in the toilet! Get ready for school now."

"Where is the bathroom?" I ask with a smile.

"You know exactly where it is, now fill up the bowl and wash."

I try to make it easier for myself. I grit my teeth and fill up the orange plastic bowl with water and wash. I stand in the warm water and scrub under my arms and stoop and wash between my legs and scrub my body all over.

"Why haven't you got a proper bathtub like normal people?" I exclaim. Wunmi clouts me round the head, and says: "I'll get rid of your fancy English habits, Dr Barnardo's isn't looking after you now."

I continue to wash while I listen to her telling me that people in England don't realize she's an educated woman. Instead they call her primitive and only offer their houses, offices and shops for her to clean.

Inside my head I'm fuming away to Annabel, telling her what does Wunmi expect if she eats with her hands and speaks funny English to her few African friends. And I'm angry this morning because I'm supposed to go to grammar school, but Wunmi applied too late.

I get dressed in my new uniform. I feel like a Sindy doll with my black beret, black blazer, and black skirt. Wunmi

knots my tie and says: "Perfect. You look like a respectable
African child now. I have a present for you." She pulls out a
black briefcase. "This is for all your new books."

My body stiffens as I catch my resentful reflection on the
side of the case. I quickly force a smile. "Thank you," I
mumble.

Wunmi smiles too.

"What about my new friends? They'll think I'm a swot."

"I'll swot you if you're not careful, you ungrateful
wretch."

We travel on the number 36 bus together. Wunmi points
out where the Queen lives, the Hilton Hotel and Speakers
Corner.

"You continue looking out the window, as you'll have to
do this journey on your own after school today."

I look down onto people going to work, the shops
opening up, and I pass a canal in the middle of London
town. After twenty minutes of travelling I begin to feel
excited, and I am happy that my new school is a long way
from home. Wunmi leaves me at the school gates and says: "I
have to get back to work. Your headmistress, Miss MacBride,
is expecting you in her office in five minutes. I'll meet you at
the bus station in Victoria at the end of the day. Just make
sure you get back on the 36 bus."

I forget to say goodbye and run into the empty
playground. My new school is a skyscraper; it has seven floors
and lots of glass windows, some of which are missing. As I
enter through the double doors, somebody has sprayed "I
woz ere" on the floor. I'm hit by the stench of cigarette butts
and there is more graffiti on the walls. I walk along the
corridor and spot a girl standing on another girl's shoulders
while she tries to remove a speaker from the wall. Beep, beep,
beep. All the doors open and hoards of girls come teeming

out. I freeze, my back stuck to the corridor wall. I've not seen so many coloured faces before. A girl double the width of me stops in front of me and says: "Eh eh! Check the briefcase."

I drop it to the floor.

"So wa appen, seen a duppy?"

"I beg your pardon?"

"Bwoy, the gal inglis ee."

"I'm sorry, I don't understand you."

"Hey, check this out. Miss Bounty na understan me. Wa yu sayin?"

"Pardon?"

"Me seh you're a Bounty. A coconut darling. White inside, Black outside. Yu na see it."

Beep, beep, beep! "Can Caroline Pincus and Marjorie Herbert come to the deputy headmistress's office immediately," the tannoy blasts out.

The girl who is double my size rushes off with two other girls, and the rest walk off to their next lesson while I'm still stuck to the wall, wet now with perspiration. My white shirt has turned grey from the black dye of my blazer. I kick my briefcase to try to make it look old. At the other end of the corridor the same two girls are still busy dismantling a second speaker. Annabel is in my head, telling me it's going to be all right. So I pluck up the courage and walk up to the two girls: "Excuse me, please. Can you tell me where Miss MacBride's office is?"

"Shit," they say together.

One of the girls, whose school tie is holding a bunch together on top of her head, threatens me with her eyes and says: "If you grass on us, your life won't be worth living."

"Please help me. It's my first day here and I'm lost."

"Welcome. But you better dump that suitcase if you want to survive in this school."

"Quick, before we get caught," hisses the other girl. She's wearing a black denim pencil skirt and a black leather jacket.

"It's that way and up some stairs." She points towards a door at the opposite end of the corridor while the other pushes the two speakers into a shopping trolley and they both run out of the school. Just as I arrive outside Miss MacBride's office, the wide girl and her two friends open the door to let me in. One by one, they file out of her office, and cut their eyes at me – shutting their eyelids, half re-opening them, while directing their eye line towards the floor.

"Hello, Miss Bounty" and then the wide girl bounces me out of the way. I try my hardest not to cry.

"Enter. You must be Pauline Charles, I've been expecting you. Welcome to Edgware Towers. Let me call for your year mistress. She's responsible for all the new first years. Take a seat." She speaks into a microphone on her desk and asks for a Mrs Lyles to come to her office immediately.

Miss MacBride dresses in twin sets and pearls. Her hair always matches her clothes. When Mrs Lyles enters, her nose twitches and she gives a big thin-lipped smile. She is tall and beautiful, with long wavy auburn hair. She is wearing a woollen suit with seamed tights and shoes that make her totter on her toes.

"This is our new girl, Pauline Charles. She's two weeks late due to her family taking a late summer holiday. But I'm sure she'll settle in quickly. There are plenty of black girls in this school."

"I'm not black, I'm coloured."

"I think she means West Indian and African girls like you, Pauline," says Mrs Lyles.

"I'm English."

"Don't worry, you'll be one of the gang in no time. I'll take you for a tour of the school."

We enter the lift where "I love Bob Marley" is scrawled across the door and a bag with all its contents is dumped all over the floor. Mrs Lyles gathers up the contents up, the door closes and we creak all the way up to seventh floor.

"Let me introduce you to your new tutor group who you will have lessons with most of the time."

We enter a classroom and some girls giggle and point at my briefcase.

"What's her name, Miss?"

"My name is Pauline Charles."

"Bwoy, she posh ee," the same girl comments.

Another asks: "Where are you from?"

"I come from a pretty village in Essex."

"Essex, they na have black people in Essex." And the whole class laughs.

I look around and more than half my class is coloured. All the white girls are sitting on one side and all the coloured girls on the other. I am terrified. I don't know which side to sit on. Mrs Lyles notices the fragile look on my face and quickly says: "I'll show you the labs." We leave the classroom and walk towards the lifts. Three girls with their backs to us are using a ruler to prize the lift doors open.

"Shouldn't you be in maths, Geraldine, Hyacinth and…?"

"Yeah, Miss, but the lift has broken down."

"Is that Mrs Lyles?" a voice calls out from the lift. The three girls leave the ruler rammed between the doors and flee.

"It's Mr Walker, the maths teacher. I think the girls have stuck me in the lift."

Mrs Lyles pulls the ruler out and nothing happens. "I hope you're not going to be like that when you get into the second or third year?"

"No, Mrs Lyles."

"Come with me, I need to sort this lift out," and she leaves me sitting in her office. Just as I'm dozing off, I can hear someone calling my name. I jump up out of my seat expecting to see Mrs Lyles, but no one is there. My name is called again, and this time it comes from the window. I walk towards it and open it up. I look down past all the seven floors and search for the person who is calling me, but nobody is around. All of a sudden my eyes become heavy and the crown of my head feels as if it's being sucked into the playground. "Thou shall not kill," Annabel whispers in my head, "no, Pauline, you can't jump."

I open my eyes and the playground is writhing with snakes. I can hear them calling out my name. I pull the window down quickly and run back to my chair. I sit and wait for Mrs Lyles as if nothing has happened.

A coloured girl called Josephine with two ring combs in her hair is picked out in my tutor group by Mrs Lyles to look after me. Some of Josephine's friends scoff at her and warn her not to chat with me, otherwise she might start speaking like the Queen. She warns me never to use the lifts and ignore the teachers when they're telling me off, then abandons me for the rest of the day.

I learn how to make cakes out of cornflakes, play hockey, and concoct explosions in chemistry all on my first day at school. The day passes so quickly that when I hear six beeps I know it's time to go home. On my way out I am stopped on every flight of the stairwell and asked, "Are you the new posh girl?", and some people say "Hello Miss Bounty" and run off laughing.

By the time I reach the school gates I'm too scared to open my mouth. The wide girl and her two friends are policing the exit. "Bring us sweets tomorrow or else." I nod my head as if to say yes and run past them at top speed to my bus stop.

I use my dinner money to bring sweets for the whole week until one day Annabel gives me an idea. She says she'll bring her friends and scare them off, but I know that could make it worse. So I invent two big brothers instead, and when Monday morning comes and they're waiting at the gates, I say: "If you don't leave me alone, my brothers Pedro and Warren will come and beat you up."

After that they never ask again. They just make me squeeze past them without touching as I go in and out of the school gates. And every time they catch sight of me, they just turn their backs and mock me by saying: "Inglis gal" under their breath.

19

I don't understand why I have to change from being English to African and coloured to black. Wunmi tries to beat the English out of me every morning before I go to school. Most mornings I forget to rub cream into my skin and she says: "What am I going to do with this English child?" before she licks me with a belt.

"I don't want you mixing with any West Indian children because they're all troublemakers, and you're not to play with English children either as they will corrupt your mind," she warns.

"But you just said I'm English."

"You brainwashed child. You're African. What have those Dr Barnardo's people done to my child?"

I leave for school feeling puzzled, not knowing who I can talk to, and how I work out who is West Indian and who isn't. I still feel English and don't want to be anything else.

At school, some girls come up to me and ask: "Why are you so black?" I sit next to Josephine in class and she says I'm black like a non-stick Teflon frying pan.

"Are you African?" she inquires.

"No, I'm English."

"You're African, that's why you're so black."

"I'm coloured like you."

"I wouldn't use the word coloured in this school. That's racism."

"What's racism?"

She looks at me as if I have two heads. "No one is coloured here, some people are burnt black like you, others are half-caste, some have crocodile skin, and some are dundus."

"But I'm the same colour as you."

She almost falls off her seat with fear and says: "No way, José. I'm a red skin." She asks me where my parents are from.

"My mother was born in Nigeria."

"See, I told you that's why you're so black. Where is your dad from?"

"Oh, he's from St Kitts," I make up. I had read about the island of St Kitts in a book and the name sounded romantic.

"Well, that's cool. But you're still half African. You better just talk about your dad while you're in this school."

I don't want to be in this school. I want to be back in the Village where nobody mentions colour and where most of us aren't sure where we really come from. Aunty Claire's voice still haunts me. As if she was standing beside me, I can hear her proudly saying we are all the same. When I ask Annabel her opinion she says: "When you come to live in heaven there will be no prejudice at all."

After three weeks I make my first friend. I meet her on the bus on my way home. She is wearing the proper school uniform but she uses her school tie as a ribbon in her brown wavy hair. Most of the girls at Edgware Towers live in West London, so I have been travelling south all on my own. So when Henrietta taps me on my shoulder and asks if she can sit next to me, I'm so excited that I want to tell her everything. But Wunmi has reinvented my life, I must tell people I have been at boarding school in a small village in Essex. I think of telling her about Annabel, but know she is best kept in my head.

Henrietta taps me on the shoulder again and says: "You must be brainy, you're always thinking. I've watched you reading on the bus most days." I can't believe she wants to speak to me and I feel overwhelmed with tears.

"What's wrong?"

"Nobody likes me."

"I do."

"What about everybody else?"

"They like you. They just think you're strange, with your posh voice, and…"

"I know they all laugh behind my back because I wear my skirts so short."

"Oh, you can sort that out. My mum used to do that to me until I started choosing pleated skirts, and now she doesn't know how to take them up."

"What about my briefcase?"

"That makes you look smart. We can swap bags if you like?"

We travel all the way to Victoria and practise counting in binary on our fingers. Henrietta gets off at a big concrete estate, but we plan to meet up at the bus station every day for school.

Every Saturday begins at 8am. I fill a bucket with a loofah, flannel, scrubbing brush, vim, soap and some dettol. I run all the way downstairs and queue in the washroom. Annabel tickles me with her breath which makes me smile when the neighbours say good morning.

"What a lovely smile you have, blossom. Where's your

mum?"

I just keep on smiling as I'm not allowed to talk to anybody.

I've learnt to speak to Annabel inside my head. When she visits, she hovers above it, and I think very hard so she can hear all my thoughts. It's a trick she taught me as soon as I moved to London. She can hear me thinking about the smell of piss, and how I want a bathroom upstairs in my flat. She says that in heaven I'll never have to worry about bathing. I tell her I can't wait to join her. By the time a bath becomes available I've got used to the idea of sharing. I like the warmth of everybody who has just finished bathing as they pass me going back upstairs. They all wear a big grin and say: "Have a lovely day." There is always a thick dirty skid mark left behind in the bath, and bits of blonde, ginger and black hair stuck down the plughole. I scrub the bath clean before Wunmi appears. She always gets into the bath first. I watch her release her breasts as they sway across her stomach. I look at her body every time she picks the soap up and rubs it into the loofah. Wunmi is happy in the bath and forgets I'm standing behind waiting to scrub her back. It's the only time I get to see her hair, a mass of black cotton wool. New wigs make her look different every month.

Once her dead skin has been scrubbed off with the loofah, it's my turn to step into the bath. I poke my big toe in and Annabel can hear my thoughts. She whispers in my ear: "Get in before it's too late." My two feet stick to the bottom, and I feel a strong hand push me down.

"Stoop," Wunmi says, and pushes a flannel between my legs, and I begin to wash everything clean. I let the water run out, and my naked body is coated with greyish suds.

"Rinse, you nasty English girl, don't bring your filthy habits here," and she fills a bucket with cold water and throws it all over me.

But every week I bring my filthy habit because I love the thrill of having cold water splashed all over me. It's so much fun that it's worth the whack on the back.

Next I rub Nivea cream all over my skin, but it sits on top of it making my skin look grey again. I rub so hard that my hands begin to ache. Wunmi leaves me alone to finish off greasing my skin. After our bath we go shopping for food for the week: pigs' trotters, liver, tripe and a boiling chicken. We buy green banana, yams and plantains from the vegetable market, and then go home to cook.

In the afternoon a pot of stew is prepared for the week. I stand by the door, watching Wunmi cook. She peels, washes and chops the onions. By the time she tosses them into a pan of sizzling oil and stirs them, my eyes are like whirlpools. A wooden spoon flies out of her hand and she screams: "African girls don't cry when their mothers peel onions." I duck and it lands on the floor. As I go to pick it up, I bite my lip to try and stop myself from answering back. But it's too late; as I hand the spoon back I blurt out: "Well, this one does."

The wooden spoon snaps on my head. I get so used to the spoons snapping that I try to guess each Saturday how many Wunmi will break on me that day. I can hardly feel them, and they never seem to stop the onion from making my eyes water. But they do stop me from speaking my thoughts out aloud.

It's my job to watch the rice. If it burns I get licks of Wunmi's belt. But I don't really care as I think rice is for poor people, especially the kind that looks like mashed potato and you eat with your hands. Yuck, I say to myself every time I have to stand by and watch the rice cook. Wunmi and I share the same plate. She pushes all the gristly bits of meat over to me, and I sit on my hands to stop myself from throwing all of it onto the carpet. By Wednesday the meat is quite tender and it becomes the best thing I've ever tasted. I'm sucking my fingers, chewing on bones, and licking the plate clean.

20

Aunty Hilma is Jamaican and very loud. Wunmi says she's different from the lazy rude barbarian West Indians she knows and that she should have been born an African. Aunty Hilma is one of the two friends Wunmi holds on to. All her other friends last one week and end up being cursed down the telephone. When we arrive at Aunty Hilma's house she is often ill and sometimes screams from her bed. If she's well, she bellows so loud that I think I'm caught in a gale. When we visit, her son Hubert always opens the door and we wait to see if we must join a small queue outside her bedroom. When Aunty Hilma screams: "Lord have mercy, give me strength," Wunmi and I take our place behind her husband, Uncle Claybourne. Hubert runs into the kitchen and fetches a bag of ice that is passed down the line to a doctor. After five minutes, the doctor reappears and says to all four of us: "It's just another bad migraine. Nothing to worry about, just try to keep her room dark."

Hubert rushes around drawing the bedroom curtains and stuffing blankets in places where he can see some light. We all sit on the edge of Hilma's bed in the dark and listen to her whimpering sermons to her dear Lord. Annabel flies from above my head to hover over Hilma, giving her some of the

Lord's strength.

When Hilma is well, her house is filled with calypso music, "rice an peas" and curried goat. It's my favourite meal once I've picked the rice out. Hubert and I play scrabble and ludo while Wunmi and Hilma shout and laugh hysterically.

A few weeks before Christmas, I hear Wunmi shouting down the phone. I wonder who is at the other end catching all her curses. I hear Hilma's name and then the phone slamming down. And I know that we will not be visiting Aunty Hilma's lively home again.

When her other friend is about to visit, I'm sent to the shops to buy Guinness and a packet of Rothmans. When the person arrives I'm sent to my room and never get to see who drinks out of the cans and smokes cigarettes with Wunmi. I listen at the door and hear a deep male voice. I imagine him to be very handsome, tall, and wearing a suit. His voice is deep and Wunmi's voice is softer. I can hear chatter and then all of a sudden they become silent. I almost jump out of my skin when there's a loud thud on the floor. It's the only time I ever hear Wunmi giggle, then her bedroom door slams shut. I begin to hear bed springs jumping up and down and heavy breathing that makes me feel very scared. I wonder if Wunmi is about to die. She lets out a big scream and I jump onto my bed, bury my head under my pillow and call for Annabel's help.

Wunmi always sings songs about Africa after her visitor has left, and she is always happy. She lets me out of my room and I get to smell his Brut aftershave and eat the Black Magic chocolates he has left behind while I tidy up the mess.

He visits on Friday evenings and has left by the time I wake up on Saturday morning. One evening while I'm listening at my bedroom door, I hear them playing with the furniture, shouting insults at each other, and then the front door slams shut. The next morning Wunmi has bruises all over her face and screams at me to clear up. There are no chocolates today and no beautiful songs, just the licks of Wunmi's belt when she catches me smelling the bits of pinstripe cloth torn off her man friend.

I never meet any more of her friends, but some nights she just disappears, coming back with a smile on her face and sometimes singing a new African song.

"Police and Thieves" by Junior Murvin is playing at the school Christmas party and my feet feel as if they're stuck in a bog. I can hardly pick them up and when I try to move my hips they jerk me around the room. My two left legs don't know how or where to move next, so they miss every beat. I've not heard reggae before and think it's fun to pogo around to the deep base beats. The black girls are sneering: "Shimmer guy, Shame." And the white girls are saying: "I thought all black people could dance."

"Hey Rock 'n' Roll" by Showaddywaddy plays next and Annabel comes with her friends to save me. They take hold of my hair and twist me around. I am bopping with the Angels and I can almost do the splits. The white girls stand in awe of me and shake my hand. They all want to know where I learnt to jive. The black girls turn their backs on me and make their own music by sucking on their teeth.

Josephine takes me to one side and says: "Wa rung wid yu? Yu na know how to dance to reggae? Why yu love up white people music dem?"

I am saved by the six beeps. It's the last day of term. I grab my bag and run as fast as I can to the bus stop, forgetting I'm meant to wait for Henrietta to travel together all the way home.

Wunmi forgets my birthday, and she forgets to come home on Christmas day. On Christmas Eve she sends me down to the bathroom for a wash, I run the bath and she doesn't turn up.

I let the water out and run back upstairs, but nobody is in so I wait on the doormat. I wait patiently, and every time I hear heels echoing up the stairs I jump up with joy, hoping she has been shopping for all my presents tomorrow. But the stomping of her high heels never comes. I fall asleep to the sound of Christmas carols blasting from other flats. The next-door neighbour wakes me up on Christmas morning and invites me into her house. My heart leaps, and then my tummy begins to feel sick; I know that Wunmi would go berserk. So I wrap the towels around me and say I'll be all right. She brings me out a leg of turkey, mince pie and a Christmas cracker, and says: "If you want to join us, you can."

I nod my head and she goes back in. I pull the cracker with both hands and out pops a rubber snake and some plastic gold coins.

I fall asleep again and wake up to the measured sound of heels clonking up the stairs. It's Wunmi's walk, I throw the food under the neighbour's mat and post the paper plate and plastic cup through the letterbox. Wunmi is wearing a brand-new blue coat and a matching bag. There is no bag of presents for me. I crawl into my bed that night and beg God to take me away. I remember the Blooms in Saviours Cottage always saying: "If you pray hard enough God will eventually answer all your prayers."

The next morning she leaves me in the house with a pot of Jollof rice, spiced turkey and the television on full volume. It feels like Christmas today as I have nobody to tell me off or beat me. She comes back late and the next morning we both wake up to an ordinary day.

In the new year a social worker has finally managed to contact Wunmi. She wants to see how I am getting on. Wunmi instructs me to smile charmingly and tell her how happy I am with my new home and school. She visits me one day after school. When the door is knocked, I call through the letterbox to ask who it is. I open the door to a tiny woman with pepper-and-salt-coloured hair. Her name is Mrs Burgess.

"That's a lovely smile you have."

"Thank you," but I don't budge an inch and keep her on the doormat.

"How are you liking living in London?"

"Fine."

"How are you getting on with Wunmi?"

"Fine."

"How are you liking your new school?"

"Fine."

What's the point of this visit? Nobody listened to me when I said I didn't want to leave the Village, and everyone said it was for the best. The only person left to confide in is God. I look at her and gulp down all my tears.

"What's wrong?" Mrs Burgess asks.

"I'm fine."

"No you're not," whispers Annabel, but I tell her it's none of her business and please get out of my head. I spread a smile over my face and Mrs Burgess says: "I'm happy you're fine, I'll come to visit you next month." I shut the door and get on with my evening chores.

I sweep the house and tidy all the rooms. I can hear

Wunmi's heels marching up the stairs, I run from room to room checking everything is in its place. The key turns and I run to the door to help with her bags. I greet her with a big nervous smile.

"Why are you smiling?"

"Because I'm fine."

"What do you mean, fine?"

"I don't know."

"What did you say to the social worker?"

"I'm fine."

"You're lying" – smash – "Don't try to defend yourself" – smash – "How dare you give me that typical English smile?" – smash. I fall to the ground. My head holds her footprints indented in my ear. Phlegm moistens the pain as she rubs my head into the carpet. I can't escape out of my body. Not even Annabel and her friends are strong enough to suck me out although they can hear me screaming inside my head for help. Some of Annabel's friends hop on top of my chest, pushing it up and down while Annabel flaps her wings, forcing air into my mouth. She watches over me while her friends wrap me in their candyfloss wings. I leave my smile in Wunmi's front room that day. Annabel tries to push it back on, but I won't let her. I never look at Wunmi's face again; my eyes stay angled at the ground.

My body finds its way into my bedroom and puts itself in bed. I'm too scared to fall asleep just in case I don't wake up. Something jumps into my bed beside me. I can hear Annabel whispering: "Float, Pauline, float." But it's too late; my body is weak and I'm beginning to lose faith in my Angel friends. I lie awake thinking that if I am a child of God, why does he let this happen to me? But I have no one else to turn to.

I imagine my Uncle George in Saviours Cottage, tucking me up for the night and telling me: "There is no need to ever worry, as the Lord is thy saviour." I lie awake waiting to be saved.

With my final piece of strength I drag myself under the blankets and begin praying to God to take me away. Murmuring from the front room disturbs my prayers. I can hear Wunmi speaking her funny English and then she slams down the phone. I close my eyes and my body feels as if all my blood has been sucked out of it. The African chief I have dreamt of stirs me in my sleep. He starts hurling all his gold and ivory at my body. Wunmi's weeping stops me from falling back into a deep sleep. I quiver beneath my sheets, waiting for her to come in. But instead she breaks down and sobs from the front room. "Please, God, what have I done to deserve this child?" She wails again: "Please forgive me."

I turn over, put my head beneath the pillow and cry "Please, God" too.

21

Henrietta says I've changed when I meet her at the bus stop in the new year. "Why are you hanging your head so low? You look like the hunchback of Notre Dame."

I shrug my shoulders, and she notices the new pair of shoes that Wunmi has chosen for me.

"Not even my granny would be seen alive wearing those. No wonder you're all hunched up. Look at your feet!"

They are black, with a big brooch and without any heels. I open my briefcase and pull out a pair of plimsolls I've managed to smuggle out of the house. I swap my shoes for my plimsolls, which half hang off my feet. Henrietta laughs as I wrap laces around the whole of my foot to keep the soles and tops sandwiching my feet in place.

"Here, we better swap bags; at least you'll look halfway trendy." I take hold of her canvas Alfred Marks bag and I begin to feel flash with my new school skirt. I took her advice and chose a pleated skirt when I went shopping with Wunmi. She compromised and settled for a skirt with pleats at the front, and it was impossible for her to take it up.

When Henrietta and I sit on the bus together, something jumps onto my lap and when I push it off, it dissolves into flickering light. "What are you doing now?" demands Henrietta.

"Nothing, I'm just arranging my skirt." I can sense Henrietta getting scared so I tell her about Christmas and her eyes almost pop out of her head. I tell her about the Christmas tree just like the one we had in Cross Cottage.

I make up a story about staying at my cousin's house and all the presents we'd opened. She wants to hear everything about Midnight Mass as her parents are atheist. My stories last all the way to school.

When we get off the bus I know that something is following me. By the time we reach school, it is sitting comfortably on my shoulder. It feels very different from Annabel; it has a heavy feeling that drags me down. It stifles all my laughter and makes me feel angry most days. I can't help being aggressive. I answer back all the teachers and call them slags. When the teachers tell me off for not concentrating, I stare so hard at my exercise book and pen on the desk that they fall onto the floor. And then I'm sent to withdrawal for my disruptive behaviour. I'm thrown out of class at least once a week. And my name becomes the headliner over the school tannoy system. Often I'm smarter than the teachers, so I answer them back and everyone thinks I'm a hero.

In history Mrs Mackintosh teaches us about Captain Cook, who discovered Australia. I tell her it's all lies and ask: "What about the Aborigines?"

"They don't count," she replies.

"You're thick just like this history book," and it flies off the table, landing at her feet.

Josephine and Marjorie, the two worst in the class, say: "Pauline's right."

"It's arl lies yu teach us. Captain Cook teef up Australia just like Christopher Columbus teef up de West Indies. That's what me mudda says," shouts Marjorie. And she picks up her history book and throws it at Mrs Mackintosh with Josephine's following swiftly behind. We're all sent to the withdrawal room and our parents are rung up and asked to come and take us home.

Josephine's sister comes to pick her up. She has worked out a scam with her sister, who lives at home with her two children, and so whenever Josephine gets into trouble, her older sister picks up the phone and pretends to be the mother. Marjorie's mother cusses her and pushes her into a car. Wunmi can't make it until after school finishes, so I'm sent home to wait.

I sit on my bed, rocking to and fro waiting for the sound of her high heels charging up the stairs. At the slam of the door, I leap to my bedroom door.

"How dare you play with those West Indian girls? What have I told you?"

I keep my eyes directed towards the ground, waiting for her next move. I can hear her thinking aloud, I'll teach her a lesson. I try to leap out of my body, but the thing on my shoulder is keeping my feet weighted down. I can feel Wunmi's eyes scratching at my forehead. She takes a swing at me and I raise my hands to defend myself. She boxes me and screams: "So you think you're Cassius Clay."

I duck and I hear Wunmi's hand land on the front room wall. My face breaks into a big smirk, but she can't see it as my eyes are fixed on the carpet. I can't hear or see what she is about to do next. I sneak a look from beneath my brow and she is standing on the sofa, pulling the curtains down. She yanks out the thin white curtain wire and walks back towards me. I begin to fly just like how Sparky taught me as a child. I take two deep breaths and I'm out of body floating above my head. I can see that the thing on my shoulder has disappeared.

I watch Wunmi order me to stick out my two wrists. She rolls each sleeve up to my elbow and says: "Don't move. If you flinch you'll get more." She whips each wrist nine times. I watch them swell as if they've caught a sudden bout of mumps. My arms change colour from dark brown to purple to red.

Annabel is holding my hand, she is pushing me towards my body but I refuse to re-enter it. She says: "Blow, go on, blow down onto your wrists." She helps me by floating down towards my flaming arms and wrapping her candyfloss body around my wrists.

She looks up at me and says, "You have to pray, Pauline." And then she tries to suck me back into my body, but I stay hovering above my head.

"You've got to come back, Pauline."

In a flash, I'm back in my body. My wrists are on fire. I can't believe how my skin has turned red. I walk into my room and force every tear back into my body. I know if I cry there will be more. My wrists hurt so much it's as if they're the only part of my body that is alive.

It's almost impossible to carry my briefcase out of the flat and down the stairs the next day. I kick it down and when it reaches the bottom, I manage to shove it under my armpit, clasping it firm all the way to the bus stop. Henrietta offers to carry my bag around the school for the whole week and a rumour spreads that Pauline has had fierce licks.

At the end of the week, Wunmi is waiting for both Henrietta and me to arrive at Victoria station. She pulls the briefcase from Henrietta's hand and demands that she take us to her parent's house. She rages all the way to Henrietta's block of flats.

Wunmi knocks on Henrietta's door, and when it opens she apologises to her mother. "I'm sorry for causing you concern, I'll make sure it never happens again."

"Not to worry. I was just concerned my daughter was being bullied."

"What do you mean, Mum?" Henrietta asks.

Her mother pulls at her daughter's hand, revealing a red mark across her fingers. "I needed to check with the school that Pauline wasn't bullying you into carrying her heavy bag."

"But I told you Pauline and I sometimes swap bags."

"Don't worry, Mrs Thomas, I'll make sure it never happens again." Wunmi unbuttons her coat, takes the belt from her skirt and whips me in the doorway.

"Pull her in," Henrietta's mother calls out to her husband.

He appears at the front door and says: "No, it might make it worse for the kid."

"Mum, Mum, do something. It's all your fault."

"It's best not to get involved," says Mrs Thomas and she pushes Henrietta indoors.

Henrietta's father says: "You better move from here, otherwise someone might call the police."

Wunmi ignores him and he slams his door on us. I can hardly feel the lashes through my blazer. When the belt whips my bare legs, I wish I hadn't turned my socks down to be fashionable like everyone else at school. A couple of Henrietta's neighbours just walk pass us both as if nothing is happening.

Wunmi eventually puts her belt in her coat pocket, drags me home by my arm and sends me straight to my room. My briefcase never closes properly after that day. I'm not sure whether it's the thing on my shoulder which made me break it, or Wunmi's fury in the middle of the street. But she never mentions the briefcase again and comes back home the next day with a satchel in her hand. It's not perfect, but at least I don't mind being seen carrying a black satchel around.

22

Fran is the only white girl in the first-year school netball team. She's one of the reserves. Most people are frightened of her because she wears a black hooded cloak and looks like a witch. Her family live in a caravan parked in wasteland near the school. Everyone knows her name as it's blasted over the tannoy every other day. So she's accepted by the troublemakers of the first year. Fran has noticed how good I am at netball and begins to shadow me around. She encourages me to come to the trials for the team as somebody has dropped out.

The coach, Miss Williams, says: "I don't care how good you are, any nonsense and you're out."

"Does that mean I'm in?"

"I need permission from your parents first before I can say yes."

Mrs Lyles manages to convince Wunmi to let me play as she thinks it will help to improve my behaviour if I'm representing the school. Wunmi buys me a new pair of plimsolls, I get picked for the first team as goalkeeper and I make a whole bunch of new friends. On the pitch we play together like clockwork, watching each other's moves, helping our goal shooters to score. We are top of the league and become known as one of the scariest teams in London. Most of us are bigger than the white girls in other teams and often they're so scared of us that they keep on dropping the ball. When we play against a predominantly black team, we cuss and kiss our teeth. And when we think we're losing, we trip up the other team to make sure we win. But the match often continues off the pitch. The girls from the losing team hang outside our school gates, picking a fight with anyone wearing the school uniform.

Fran grabs me one day while I'm getting ready for practice. "What's your cat's name?"

"My cat?"

"Yes, your cat. I can see her perched on your left shoulder."

I stop tying my plimsolls and jerk myself up. And there on my left shoulder is a ball of brown fur.

"You better give her a name; otherwise she might never leave you."

"What do you mean?"

"It will try to steal your body if you're not careful. Meet me in the gym tomorrow at lunchtime. I'll explain then."

I tell Miss Williams that I feel too sick to train at netball practice tonight and ask if I can go home. She makes me sit and watch as she says this is part of training too. I can feel my ball of fur clinging onto my shoulder, making me feel even sicker.

The next day I meet Fran in the gym; she is waiting with a couple of other girls from the second year. Patsy and Eileen are best friends and almost look like twins with their Jackson Five Afros and matching school bags. They've been the talk of the school as they've just recently returned after both giving birth. One of the boys from the neighbouring school got Patsy up the duff. And it's rumoured that Eileen's dad got her pregnant. She's not been the same since Social Services took her baby off her because of its severe ill mental health and physical handicap. Lara, who is new to the group too, wears a ponytail to her waist, with a fringe that almost drowns her face. Everyone knows that she lives in a home because her parents were both in the papers for smuggling drugs. They got sentenced to ten years in prison.

I shiver as I notice that all of us have big balls of fur perched on our shoulders. Fran catches my nerves on edge and quickly welcomes Lara and me to the group.

"I need to go to the toilet," says Lara.

"Don't you want to find out who your cat is?" asks Fran.

"Yes."

"Well you better hang round for a while." Fran turns to me and asks: "So do you know who your cat is?"

"No."

"What, you don't know how it died?"

"But I'm alive."

"No, not you," says Patsy.

"I'm not sure then."

"Well, you better find out soon, otherwise you'll end up dying the same way as that cat who is sitting on your shoulder," Fran warns.

Lara shudders and confesses that she doesn't know how her cat died. Fran asks us what we both dream about. "I dream of falling. Yes, I'm always falling," I answer.

"You must have been impatient."

"How did you work that out?"

"Because people only fall when they're greedy for something. They're too impatient to wait for what they want to come to them."

Lara announces proudly that she dreams about spiders all the time.

"Spiders! You're trapped," exclaims Eileen.

"Trapped! What do you mean?"

"Spiders need their webs, just like we need our bodies. The difference is we get trapped. That's what my mum says. I was trapped in my body for three years. A machine kept me alive at birth. When they finally switched it off I was so mad that in a week I was back inside my mother's body. You see, I couldn't let go. And now I have this cat who died in a similar way and wants to live in my body."

Fran butts in and asks, "Shall I show you how your cat died?"

I say yes without thinking.

We find an empty changing room and close the door. Fran instructs me to lie on a bench while she stands at my head and Lara at my feet. Patsy and Eileen stand either side and I close my eyes. Fran pushes my cat off my shoulder and I can feel the weight of it curled up on my tummy. Fran's fingers are on my temples and she instructs the others to place their fingers lightly under my body.

She hypnotically says: "Now all repeat after me. Accident. Car crash. Through the window screen. Glass. Blood. Ambulance. You're dead, dead." She murmers: "Now raise her with one finger from each hand."

My body jolts through a shaft of cold air, and I can't hear my new friends speaking anymore. My body feels as if it's weightless as it glides towards a breeze of warm air. I know it's not heaven because Annabel and her friends are not waiting for me. I pass Sparky and Bobby as I carry on travelling upwards towards a bright light. And then a sudden blast of fire passes by me at great speed and I can see my black cat crumpled in a heap at the foot of a block of flats. The cat begins to move. At the moment it lifts its head, I am staring at a twelve-year-old girl who has jumped off a high rise.

"Give me your body," she pleads with her bloody hands stretched out.

"No."

"Please. I'll look after it."

"No. I'm not ready to die."

"Yes, you are. I watch you every day asking God to take you away," and then she rushes towards my body.

"No," I scream.

And my body falls so fast, landing back on the bench, and I wake up to a cup of water thrown into my face

"So, do you know who your cat is?"

"I don't know her name. But I think I know how she died."

"Patience. It's a start."

Lara calls out, let me have a go, but the three beeps go for the afternoon lessons. "See you all here tomorrow lunchtime," Fran says.

We meet in the gym at exactly the same time the next day. Fran lets me be the guide as Lara lies down on a bench and prepares to find out how her cat died. "Let your cat do the talking," Fran says to me. My voice becomes soft like a whisper, and my cat tells the other girls to repeat after it: accident, high rise, on the top floor, at the window, jump, jump, falling, falling, dead, the girl at the window is dead. Lara rises above our fingers; she is weightless and hovers quite high, bobbing around in midair. We guide her back to the table by pulling lightly at her arms and legs.

"One, two, three, wake up," Fran shouts, but there is no movement. One of the other girls runs to the bogs for a cup of water. She throws it over her, but still Lara doesn't move.

"What's happened to her cat?" I ask. And in the same instant she jumps up off the bench and runs out of the gym all the way up to the seventh floor. All four of us follow and, as she reaches the seventh floor, she passes out. A teacher comes to our rescue and sends Lara off to hospital.

We all stare at each other and go off to our next lesson. The headmistress's voice interrupts the end of my science lesson. "Pauline Charles, Fran Irons, Patsy Quinine and Eileen Knuckles, come to the headmistress's office immediately."

Miss MacBride's nose is twitching and I wonder if she can see our cats. Fran's ball of fur seems double the size, and Patsy's looks like a hedgehog.

"What's all this about black magic in the gym?" I can feel my cat clawing at my shoulders and I know everyone else can too. None of us answer. Fran shuffles her feet, while I dig my hands deep down into my blazer pocket; the others twist the sleeves of their school cardigans into knots. After the silence Miss MacBride says: "This is serious. A pupil of mine is ill in hospital. What did you do to her?"

"We were just playing, Miss. Honest," says Patsy.

"You'll all be punished for this, I will be sending a letter to your parents in this evening's post. Now get back to your lesson, and no more of this black magic nonsense."

As we empty out of the headmistress's room, Eileen turns to Fran and says: "It's all your fault, my cat was fast asleep, until I met you."

"Well, now it's awake you can tell it to piss off and go find someone else."

Eileen scowls at her and says: "So what do we tell our parents?"

"Wake up early to catch the post, you'll know which one it is. It will come in a brown envelope. They always do."

I rush out of school as soon as the six beeps go. I manage to catch the early bus and travel home on my own. I feel sick and go to bed early. I fall asleep wondering why my cat has chosen me. I'm frightened that it might try to steal my body in my sleep, so I ask Annabel to watch over me. But she forgets and I wake up fighting with my blankets. Wunmi is towering over me, brandishing a belt in one hand and a brown envelope in the other. And I can see my cat sitting at the end of my bed.

"What do you know about Obia?" Wunmi demands.

"Who's Obia?" I ask.

She pulls me out of bed and orders me to strip. Wunmi douses me with a spray that smells of garlic and then tells me to bend. I bend like a robot.

"You're to stay touching your toes until you tell me who told you about Obia." She whips me across the back of the knees and leaves me doubled up while she fixes her breakfast before work.

As she leaves she says: "You're to stay touching your toes until I get back from work. This way, the evil Spirits will fall out of your head." As soon as she leaves I put my nightie on, run to the bin and find the letter Miss MacBride has sent to my home. I'm suspended for one week and I'm not allowed to practise black magic anymore.

I crawl into bed with a dictionary and look up the words black magic and Obia. I can only find black magic – it says people who use magic for evil purposes to invoke the devil. I wonder if the cat on my shoulder is the devil. Maybe that's why God hasn't answered my prayers yet. I try pulling it off, but it won't move, its claws are dug deep into my left shoulder. I make a pact with myself to start praying every night again. I tell myself if I do this and stop playing with Fran, God will definitely answer my prayers. I go back to bending over and touching my toes. Maybe Wunmi is right. I'm full of evil Spirits that get me into trouble.

When she returns at lunchtime, she says: "You can get

dressed now. This should have doused your brain."

"Can I have something to eat?" I ask.

"The only thing you'll be eating for the next week is bread and water to help cleanse that wicked soul of yours." She slams the bedroom door shut, and marches back out to work.

23

In the kitchen is a box of Thornton's peanut toffee which has been standing on the sideboard for over month. In the week I'm suspended from school, I take one piece of toffee to go with every meal. By the end of the week, I go to the box and there are only three pieces left. My heart misses a beat. I count one, two, three several times before realising that there are no more to be found. I convince myself that Wunmi must have eaten some. Too terrified to eat another whole piece, I cut a sliver from all three toffees left in the box.

The day before I'm allowed back to school Wunmi calls me into the kitchen and asks me if I want a piece of toffee. I say yes and she tells me to open the box. There are none left and I panic.

"Where is the toffee?" Wunmi asks me.

"I don't know."

"Don't lie." And she pushes my head towards the empty box, smashing it down on the sideboard. "That will knock the devil out of you. Now, get to bed and make sure you're ready for school tomorrow morning."

I meet Henrietta the next day at the bus stop and I know she is scared of me. But she wants to know all that happened in the gym with the second years. I tell her that I can't remember and so we travel silently to school.

I bump into Lara as soon as I enter the school. She says: "Thanks for the other day. I know who my cat is," and runs off in the opposite direction. Fran's mother stops her from coming to netball practice. And whenever I bump into Patsy and Eileen, we just nod at each other and walk the other way. We are all too scared to talk anymore about our cats and we never meet up in the gym again. In two weeks we're breaking up for the summer holiday.

I miss Henrietta and Josephine, but it's great not having to go to school for six whole weeks and not think about logarithms, hypotenuses, Henry the Eighth and all the bloody battles Britain fought. I get to stay indoors all day long and after my chores Annabel and I go flying across London. I look down on top of the Queen's Palace, fly over Pigeon Shit Square and, when we get to St Paul's Cathedral, I ask Annabel if we can stop to go to the loo. But she ignores me and we keep on flying over water, railway tracks and farms until we arrive at my old home the Village. And I get to see Terry and Pedro playing long jump in the sandpit on the kinder green. Annabel never lets me land because she says I'll frighten them away. So I just look at my old friends and wish I could stop and stay. Osmond walks out of Cross Cottage and I try getting back at him for all the horrid things he forced me to do by peeing down on him, but the clouds catch all my piss, and Annabel says it's time to go home.

During the holidays Wunmi lets me start a paper round early in the morning. She says we need some extra money for a big surprise. I'm excited, I think it means we are going on a holiday to Africa, and, if I save hard enough, a new pair of shoes for school. I don't mind that the bag digs into my shoulder and the papers make the palms of my hands black. While I walk from door to door, run down into basements along Tachbrook Street, and weave in and out of the streets which link it up to Belgrave Road, I hear again all the songs that Wunmi has sung about Africa and can't wait to go flying in a plane.

At the end of my first week, my dream of visiting Africa changes into something even better. Wunmi says I have to give her all my money because I have an eighteen-year-old sister coming to live with us in England.

This is better than I could ever imagine, a new big sister. Her name is Ade Shola and she lives in Nigeria with her granny. Wunmi says we need all the money we can earn to pay for her flight, college books, warm clothes and a new bed. I help Wunmi in her evening job too, cleaning offices every night, so we have enough money for my new sister when she arrives. I become too busy to go flying with Annabel to see my friends in the Village and all I can think about is the sister I'm about to meet. Every night after work I ask Wunmi if she has arrived. She smiles and says the plane is not ready to bring her yet. We don't buy a new bed. Instead I swap rooms with Wunmi and gain a double bed.

My summer holidays have finished and Ade Shola still hasn't arrived. And I'm getting tired from delivering papers seven mornings a week and cleaning offices for six, with school piled in between. Wunmi buys me a new skirt with pleats all around and says it's a present for being a hard worker. Everyone is wearing pleated skirts in the second year so I feel extremely proud.

I get a surprise when I first meet Ade Shola because she isn't dark like me and I wonder how she can be a real African with such red skin. "Are you really African?" I inquire.

"Watin," she quickly replies.

"Pardon."

"You no sabi talk pidgin English?" she says slowly.

"No but I can understand it, Wunmi speaks it most of time on the telephone."

"Le me teach you. Watin be your full name?"

"Pauline Joy Charles."

"So you be really Englisho."

"Yes, I have Wunmi's last name."

"I'm Ade Shola Olu Rotimi Femi Ajodi. Abi Princess, pikin way comot for Yoruba Cheifdom," and she lifts her battered trunk up onto our bed, smiles and says "You de follow me?"

"A chief. Does that make me a princess too?"

"No! My papa no belong to you."

"So you're my half sister."

"Half sister watin that?"

"Different dads."

"For Africa we no get half sisters or quarter sisters. We be all sisters. Call me Shola ego easier for you."

Shola begins to shiver.

"What's wrong?"

"I de coldo."

"Let's get into bed, you can unpack your things tomorrow."

I make her a hot water bottle and say: "Welcome to England."

"Watin that?"

"A bottle to keep you warm."

"English people dem ridiculous. Abi nor de sleep wid bottlo."

"Okay, freeze to death then."

Shola jumps as if she has just seen a ghost and says:

"People dem de freeze to death for England? Me no one

day read bout that for school. Watin make it so coldo?"

"Cold! You wait for winter."

She grabs the bottle and jumps into bed with all her clothes on. I roll to the edge of our bed.

"Oh God you're so Englisho. You no lek to sleep with your sister?"

Despite my embarrassment at her outburst, I cuddle up to her. Her eyelids flop down. She doesn't have a cat on her shoulder and there are no Angels hovering above her head. I look at her caramelized lean body. Shola is tall and very beautiful and has three little lines on each cheek just like Wunmi. Just as I am about to touch her cheeks, she flicks open her eyes and teases me again with "Englisho".

We chuckle and she continues to talk late into the night, telling me stories about the sun shining every day. She is so excited to be living here with her mother in England. She says: "You sabi luckio."

"Lucky, how did you work that out?"

"Me mama choose to look after you, den send you a boarding school. E traditional for le dem spoil the young one. Now my go."

I pull the covers over my head and think perhaps she's right. Maybe I am lucky. I feel lucky today to have a new sister to share my room. Shola says: "I tire," and rolls over to try and sleep.

"Me too."

I fall asleep smelling Africa on her skin. Listening to her sing-song words serenading my ears. I dream of Shola's village, Oshogbo, where the earth is always bright red. Of the river Goddess Oshun who is the mother of the human race. I can see big houses with gardens and corrugated iron houses too. And the smell of sewage fills the air. Along the dusty tracks are tall electric pylons everywhere I look until I reach the bush with its trees and small farms. I dream of mangoes, coconuts, and oranges hanging from the trees. Of the market square where women are balancing all their shopping on their heads. Men sit at the roadside selling palm wine. I am a daughter of a chief living in the same village as Shola.

On Sundays my father dresses in a silk white sokoto that flows around his legs, a matching buba buttoned to his neck, with a bright yellow agbada cloaking him from shoulder to foot. He walks beside my mother giftwrapped in colours of oranges and green from head to toe. They take me in the cloth from Oke, wrapped upon my mother's back to be blessed in the river Oshun. The wrapper that is holding me slips and I fall, head-first through the river into a jungle filled with palm trees. I can hear my mummy screaming for me. But it's not me anymore, it is the laughing chief who visits me in my dreams who is falling. Just as he is about to land in a pit of snakes, I scream out aloud: "Ayeoo!"

I wake up Shola and instead of giving me a hard time, she runs her fingers through my hair and says: "My pikin sister not so English. Your ancestors dem visit you. Ayeoo this means the world is against you. Watin be you dream?"

"Ancestors! More like you've messed up my hair."

Before Shola can say anything else, Wunmi is calling out: "Pauline, get up. You're late for your paper round."

I jump out of bed, put on my school clothes and run out of the house before Wunmi can drag me back and demand that I wash myself clean. It feels like I'm on holiday, Wunmi is happy and the sun is shining. I notice a picture of starving children from Africa on the front page of the newspaper as I put it through a letterbox. I don't look at any more papers this morning because I don't want to destroy Shola's stories or last night's dream.

Henrietta is well impressed that my sister is a princess.

As soon as she hops off the bus she spreads it round the second year before I've even entered our classroom. "Africans na have princesses," says Josephine. "They're too darn primitive for dat. Dem still climb trees and are well magre." Femi, one of my classmates, gives one of her famous lectures: "You West Indians are the inferior ones. At least my people weren't taken as slaves. My mother says West Indians have no culture whatsoever. I'm proud to be an African princess."

Before she can finish her speech, Josephine throws a punch. Femi manages to dodge out of the way.

"You Boo Boo, I'll get you at breaktime," screams Josephine. Some of the other girls divert her attention and begin talking about my hair. They're all envious of the cane row zigzagging across my head.

Every Monday my hairdos reach the gossip columns as my mates wait to inspect what Shola has created on my head. I show off cane row, inside-out corn row and china bumps. My fashion stakes have gone up.

24

Shola has been in England for two months and is already talking about going home to Africa. She complains that the streets are filthy and the English people are rude. She's had six fights with Wunmi already and most of our crockery has been smashed.

Today when I come home from my newspaper round Wunmi is banging on the toilet door. "It's been eight weeks and your period still hasn't arrived." Shola doesn't reply. "If you came to England pregnant you can get rid of the child right now."

"I de see me period," Shola yells.

"Don't flush the toilet until I've checked." Shola flushes the toilet and when she comes out Wunmi grabs her by the throat and calls her a whore. She rips all her clothes off and shouts: "I'm not having a prostitute living in my house."

Shola has a screaming fit, throwing anything she can put her hands on at the wall. "I de lef before I go crase like you." Wunmi punches her in the stomach. "Shut your dirty mouth. You're not fit to leave pikin for me house."

Shola leaps at Wunmi and they fight from room to room like two dogs. I grab my satchel and head back out to school. When I return home, Shola is not there, and I know something has happened. I wonder if Annabel has frightened her away. Annabel's not been around lately because she is jealous of my sister and says the house has become too violent for Angels to stick around. I can feel my cat trying to suck out my energy, but I've learnt to cross my legs and arms and wait until its grip slackens.

My cat jumps in front of me, with its hairs standing on end, and I know she knows that I'm getting ready to leave my body which will give her a chance to jump inside me.

Wunmi storms through the door and demands to know where Shola has gone. "You're not leaving this house, until you tell me where she is." She tugs me by the ears and pushes me to the floor. I'm out of my body so fast that I can't feel her stiletto heels pounding into my ribs. When she's finished, I jump back inside before my cat gets there first. Giving into the pain, I drag myself off to bed. In my prayers tonight I ask God why Shola didn't take me with her. I can't hear him answer, but Annabel is speaking in my head. She tells me to continue being a good girl and God will make sure my turn comes soon. I wake up to Wunmi on the telephone telling my second year mistress, Mrs Squires, that my big sister is ill, and that I need to stay at home to look after her.

Wunmi locks me in the flat when she goes out to work and I stay in bed praying to God to make Shola come back. It takes forty-eight hours for God to answer my prayers. Shola turns up on the second night, very hungry and tired. I'm so excited with my praying, that I'm hoping God will come and rescue me soon.

The evening after Shola arrives back home, Wunmi takes me downstairs to the flowerbed in the courtyard. There are two girls balancing on the bricked perimeter, walking round and round, trying their hardest not to fall off. As soon as they notice Wunmi and me they fall off, pick themselves up, and run as fast as they can into their block of flats. Wunmi sits me down on the brick wall and looks directly into my eyes. I shudder and before I have time to get panicky she is pulling a Bible out of her bag. She places it on my lap and says: "You are not to trust Shola at all. She is evil and dabbles in Obia. Do you understand?"

I kick my heels against the wall, staring at the litter on the ground. Wunmi grabs the Bible before it falls and tells me to copy her. I put one hand on my heart, the other on her Bible and repeat after her: "Dear Lord, I have sinned. Please cleanse my soul and protect me from my demonic sister Shola. I will never tell her anything about what I've just been told, and will never talk about my past. If I do, the devil will strike me down." Then Wunmi throws sage all over me and leads me back upstairs.

Shola and I stop talking for a week, until one day when I return from school she has the courage to ask me what is wrong.

"Wunmi says you're a wicked witch."

"A witch?"

"I've sworn on the Bible not to tell you anything."

We both hear a click and jump up of our bed, ready for Wunmi's entrance. But nobody is at the door. Shola, says: "She for de in house already." And she goes in search of her.

"Pauline?"

I enter Wunmi's bedroom and Shola is holding a tape recorder in one hand and a cassette in the other.

"I no believe, she de tape we conversation."

"What am I going to do now? The devil will strike me down."

"No worry. I go put other tape in."

"But she'll know."

Shola convinces me everything will be all right, and I tell her what happened in the courtyard last week. We're the best of friends again and Wunmi is suspicious.

Wunmi and Shola seem to fight almost every day, and I've been rationed to a beating every other week. Shola and I become close, and I begin to pick up her post from the postman in the morning before Wunmi gets a chance to read it. I take a bigger paper round so that Shola and I can have a little extra money. The round seems to get longer and longer so that one day it almost makes me late for school. When I return to the shop to dump my sack, my cat is sitting in the doorway and I can't move my feet to enter the shop. I can hear Wunmi's voice exploding in the shop. I stop breathing and my cat is back on my shoulder. I don't know whether to enter the shop or not. Annabel says I should go in, but since Shola ran away I realise I could do the same. Shola has promised me that she won't leave me behind again, but says: "We can't go until we save some money." She got very cold sleeping on the streets and had to eat out of people's bins. Josephine has said that my sister and me can sleep at her house if things get really tough. But I'm not sure if it's the best thing to do. At least if I keep on praying to God, he will come to my rescue one day. And Wunmi warned me when Shola disappeared that if I ever did the same, she would come and find me at Dr Barnardo's and leave me with two broken legs so I couldn't run off again.

Annabel is right: I should enter the shop. But before I do, Wunmi bumps into me on the way out.

"Here's the lying toad," she calls back into the shop.

The manager appears and says: "Your mother has been worried about you. Why didn't you tell her about the extra work?"

She takes a belt from her bag and beats me on the street. My body hits the pavement. Wunmi starts kicking me, and asks me what I've done with all the extra money.

Nobody comes to my rescue. I pick myself up with blood dripping from knees, hang my head in shame, and hope there is nobody around who will recognise me. Wunmi makes an arrangement with the manager for him to pay my wages directly to her. So that's the end of fish and chips and the odd Coca Cola on the way home from school.

The postman is early one morning and when I get back from my rounds, Wunmi is opening the post. Shola comes out of the kitchen and grabs at a letter. "Na me own. Give it back to me!"

Wunmi punches her and she falls to the ground. She kicks her like a football and says: "I can do whatever I like. It's my home."

Shola manages to pick herself up from the floor, and Wunmi runs into the kitchen, grabbing a carving knife. Shola picks up a radio and throws it, knocking the knife from Wunmi's hand. "That's it," Wunmi shouts. "I'm sending you back home." Wunmi gets on the phone and calls the police. Shola runs into the toilet and tries to barricade herself in. My cat is off my shoulder and I follow her and force my way into the toilet. Shola is sitting on the toilet with the carving knife in one hand and a bottle of cleaning fluid in the other. "Annabel!" I scream inside my head and she comes to help me knock everything out of Shola's hands. Shola puts her head in her lap and cries. My cat is on the floor rolling between us, not knowing which is the best body to borrow.

"Pauline, fetch your sister's clothes," Wunmi shouts. And my cat jumps back on my shoulder while I do as I am told.

A loud knock bangs at the door. "Let them in," Wunmi calls out to me. I open the door and three policemen charge in. I point to the living room where Wunmi is still ranting and give Shola her clothes. She is doubled up in exactly the same position.

Wunmi screams at the police: "Take her. She's an illegal immigrant. She's overstayed her visa."

Shola shouts: "It's her idea be that." The police knock on the toilet door and ask if Shola will come with them to the police station. I'm sent off to school, and told to clean up the mess when I arrive back. It's calm at home, Wunmi has no energy left to tell me off, and so I'm left to my own devices.

Shola is back in three days. The police release her on bail on the condition that she signs at the police station every day. The police tell Wunmi that Shola is to stay there until they have investigated the whole story. Nobody talks very much. I work out a way to spend more time at netball matches and rallies every other Saturday. The house has become a desert. All the pictures have fallen off the walls, there are no ornaments left on the mantelpiece, and our broken television and gramophone have been dumped outside.

25

For two weeks there is an unspoken peace truce in our home. I've counted every day that has passed without anybody fighting or being beaten. It's so serene that I think the Lord has answered part of my prayer. Even my cat has been fast asleep on my shoulder during the past fortnight. But when the second Sunday evening arrives, Shola and I know that the world record for non-violence in our home is about to be smashed. Shola and I both know something is up by the way Wunmi stomps up the stairs and opens the front door after a night out. The door slams shut and she walks straight into the kitchen. Seconds later she is in our bedroom holding an empty packet of cakes, wanting to know who ate the last one.

"Pauline, I know it's you."

"It's not me. I haven't eaten anything."

"Don't lie. All the rice has gone which I left you two for dinner yesterday."

"I mean the cake."

"If you didn't eat it, who did?"

Shola says: "Noto me."

"African children don't lie to their parents. Strip." Wunmi looks at me and I can see through my brow that she is talking to me. My cat is off my shoulder, double its size, wide awake and staring me in the face. I slowly take my clothes off.

"I'll ask you one more time: did you eat the cake, Pauline?"

"No!"

Once I'm naked, she places me in the living room, turns the paraffin heater off, and tells me to bend and touch my toes. "You can stay there until you tell the truth. Obviously not all your evil spirits have fallen out." She turns the light out and closes her bedroom door for the night.

"Please take my body," I whisper to my cat.

The ball of fur falls from my shoulder, bouncing on the floor really high. It spirals around my body. I stand up to let her jump me, but Shola frightens it away. She is at our bedroom door, begging me to come to bed. I say no, and so she chucks me a blanket for the night.

I hear Wunmi get up in the morning, and I jump up into position, forgetting all about the blanket Shola gave me last night. She opens her bedroom door and says: "Your knees are bent," and lashes me behind my knees with a piece of curtain cord. "I know you've been sleeping," and pulling the blanket away from beside my feet, gives me another lash.

It's impossible to stay bending over with my knees straight, but I grit my teeth and do my best.

"You're not going to school until you tell the truth. How dare you lie to your mother?" And she follows her words with another lick. "Go to your room and don't come back out until you are prepared to get down on your knees and beg for my forgiveness."

A tut pops out from the tip of my tongue and she whips me until I can't stand on my feet anymore.

"You're the curse of Lucifer," she shouts, picks up her bag, and marches out to work, leaving me to languish in hell.

Shola tells me to let go of my pride and do what Wunmi asks. But I refuse to budge. "I didn't do anything. Why should I beg forgiveness for something I didn't even do?"

"Africa really de inside your bellyo, your to proud," Shola replies. And my cat just sits on my shoulder waiting for my next move. I lie in bed until Shola gets back home from college and picks me up to help Wunmi with her evening job.

When we get home, I go to the bedroom. On the third evening, the phone rings and I can hear Wunmi talking. Shola comes in and tells me it's my year mistress ringing up to find out where I am. "She's not going to let you out of the house until you admit it was you."

"What about you, why don't you tell the truth?"

Wunmi calls me before Shola can answer, and hands me the phone, saying Mrs Squires wants to speak with you.

"Yes," I say.

"Are you okay?"

"Yes."

"Please do what your mother says."

I am silent. "Pauline, are you still there?"

"Yes."

"I have to get you out of the house."

"Yes."

"I can't help you until you get to school."

"Yes."

"Please do what your mother says."

I am silent again. Wunmi snatches the phone from me and I return to my room. I'm scared. I've not felt this fear before. My body feels as if it belongs to the cat one moment and to Wunmi the next, and I don't recognise my thoughts. I hate everything in sight, I want to throw everything, including myself up against the walls. Shola pushes me to the bedroom door and I walk out to Wunmi, who is still sitting beside the phone. I get down on my knees and Annabel whispers inside my head: "Please forgive me for telling a lie."

"Louder," Wunmi yells.

I can't speak any louder and I'm left kneeling, wondering what to do next. I begin to get up and Wunmi pushes me back down, yelling out: "I said louder."

I say to myself: "Go on, Pauline, you can do it. Say it louder." I can't escape my body; blinding light surrounds it as I hold my breath, count up to ten, and look at the stains on the carpet. Through gritted teeth I say: "I beg your forgiveness. I'm sorry for telling a lie."

Wunmi spits in my face and says: "When will you stop listening to all your white friends and start listening to me? The staff in the Village and now the teachers at this school have all indoctrinated your mind."

I don't move, I wait for her to spit again, but she doesn't.

"Go to your room and get your clothes ready for school tomorrow morning."

I wake up for my paper round, but when I arrive the manager says I've lost my job. "You coloureds cause me too many problems." He throws a fiver at me and says: "I'm sorry. But your mother is barking mad."

I daren't face Wunmi with the news before I go to school, so I dash off to meet Henrietta, who is waiting for me at the bus stop. As soon as she spots me coming towards her she rushes up and asks what's wrong.

"Oh, the usual." She tells me there are rumours spreading around the school that my mother gives me fierce licks.

"Well, you should know. The rumours could have only come from you."

"That's not fair." And we don't talk anymore on the bus. I arrive at school and before I can begin any lessons, Josephine is on my case, telling me Mrs Squires is on the warpath for me, and wants to know what action she's missed out on.

I avoid Josephine's questions and go to Mrs Squire's office; she takes me to the headmistress's room. "Pauline, we're putting you back in care," says Miss MacBride.

"No."

"It's not safe for you there."

"What about my sister?"

"She's an adult."

"No. Where I go, she comes too. We've made a pact," and I run out of her office, find Josephine and bunk off school for the rest of the day. I make sure I get the earlier bus so I don't have to explain to Henrietta where I've been.

I wake up the next morning to catch the post, but no brown envelope turns up to tell Wunmi I've been missing from school. Wunmi just fumes all weekend, complaining how useless I am because I have lost my early morning job. And she sends me off to school on Monday with a small bump on my forehead.

"What's that on your head?" Henrietta points out.

"I fell off my roller skates."

"You never told me you had a pair of roller skates."

"Well, I have now."

"Is that from your mum?"

"No!"

Henrietta is silent and knows not to ask any more questions.

I'm sent to withdrawal room for falling asleep in maths after PE, and in the afternoon, Josephine and I get put on report for starting a food fight in cookery. Beep, Beep, Beep. "Pauline Charles, come to Miss MacBride's office immediately."

"Why just Pauline?" Josephine demands to know. I don't

wait for an answer from the cookery teacher. I run out of class and jump into the lift. My cat jumps onto my feet, its hair standing on end. I panic. Wunmi must be waiting for me with Miss MacBride. I try to press the lift to go back up, but it's too late. The door opens and Mrs Squires is waiting for me to come out. I follow her into the headmistress's office, where there is a man sitting, wearing thick-rimmed glasses perched on the end of his nose. He smiles at me as if he knows me.

"This is Mr Jacobs from Social Services," says Miss MacBride. "You're not going home today."

"Yes I am."

"It's out of my hands. It's become a matter for the police."

I look at Mrs Squires. "But you promised."

"I'm sorry, Pauline, but I had to report your story. The PE teacher was most disturbed by the marks on your body this morning."

"I'm not going."

"It's okay. I'm going to take you somewhere safe," says Mr Jacobs.

Mrs Squires hands me my bag and coat and gives me a hug, saying it will be all right.

Mr Jacobs and I drive in silence to his office. He puts me in a room with books and toys and tells me to sit there while he does all the necessary paper work. The next time he comes in I'm fast asleep with my head on the table. He wakes me up to say: "I have a visitor for you, if you want to see her."

He takes me into another room and Wunmi is crumpled up in a chair.

She stretches her arms out to me and says: "Please come back. Shola and I need you." But I've crossed the line and I'm too frightened to go back. God has finally answered my prayers. I can feel her eyes piercing me; I glance up at Wunmi and can hear her accusing me of being a traitor.

She steals my gaze. I'm flooded with guilt. I try to leave my body, but every time I take a deep breath to help me fly, the gold coins and the ivory from my dreams are weighing my body down. All I can do is look away. Wunmi breaks down and says: "What have I done to deserve this cruel day?"

Snake

26

When I arrive at my new home I refuse to get out of the car. I point to a greyish-looking office block and ask Mr Jacobs "What's that?"

"It's your new home."

"That's not a children's home. It looks like a prison. Take me back to Wunmi and Shola now."

"I don't think that would be advisable. Now come on. This is a short stay place. At the most you'll be there for six weeks."

"Right, six weeks it is. And then I'm off." I'm still not convinced that it's a children's home with bars caging all the basement and ground-floor windows.

"Hi, I'm Roger," a stocky man with a jet-black beard like a goat's, greets me at the front door.

"Don't I have to call you Aunty or Uncle?"

He laughs, "Everyone is called by their first name here. Except of course for the head and deputy head of the home. And even the staff call them by their surnames." He notices I look worried and tries to make jokes to cheer me up. "I'm the one who should be unhappy. I've missed last orders at the pub tonight, now that you've arrived."

It takes half an hour to go through all the questions. When he finishes, he smiles and says: "I've got a problem. You're too old for the under-12s wing and too young for the adolescent unit. Which floor do you think you should be on?"

"Adolescent, I've just turned thirteen."

"Okay, it's a deal."

He hands me over to the night nurse, who shows me to my room. As soon as she's gone, I turn the light out and get into bed fully clothed. I cry for the first time, letting it spill over into my first night of a new life. I lie awake thinking that if God really loved me, why did he take so long? Now that God has rescued me, I'm not sure what I need to pray to him for. I am so mad with God for taking so long to answer my prayers, that I shut him out of my life. He's Annabel's friend not mine. I don't want to listen to Annabel anymore, and I'm definitely not praying to God.

When I wake up the next morning in my new home, something has changed. I'm in charge of my life now, and no one is going to tell me what to do. I'm old enough to look after myself.

I don't have to go to school in the morning. Instead I am introduced to my new home. There are four floors. In the basement are the laundry, kitchen and dining room, and some of the staff sleep down there too. The next floor is my unit where the older kids play games, watch TV, and go to school; the young kids live on the first floor, and us older ones sleep on the top floor with some more of the staff.

The boss, Mr Martin, walks round with a cigar in his mouth and four poodles yapping at his feet. His wife, the matron, is a sturdy woman who looks after all the cleaners, the cook and the finances. The deputy, Mr Harrington, bounces up and down on tiptoes with his hands stuffed in his trousers, playing pocket billiards all day long. And when he bounces along the corridor, the girls scream and run the other way. The staff are aged between eighteen and thirty; some of them are bikers, into heavy metal and they blast Pink Floyd and the Rolling Stones from their rooms when they're off duty.

It's all girls who live on my floor and most of us are black. Nearly everyone has been kicked out of school and are in the home for shoplifting, beating up their parents, absconding from home and truanting. I'm the only one who hasn't been in trouble with the police, but we're all waiting on court reports to decide our futures and to tell us where we have to live next.

The cook, Maud, looks like everyone's gran. She has grey hair and walks with a struggle. But everyone is terrified of her, including all the staff. She drills all of us to queue outside her meal hatch with a plate in our hands, then chucks the food on our plates and looks at us so fiercely that nobody complains. When she drops the food on the floor, she picks it up and puts it back on our plates with a smile. Sometimes when we come down to dinner at the weekend, her skittle legs are found poking out of the kitchen door, an empty bottle of Bells lying by her side. The staff tell us to halt while they tiptoe around her body, prop her up, and check to see that she's still breathing. Then they make sure there are no more bottles hiding in the toilet cistern or the oven.

Most people come for a night or two, while a few of us become temporary permanent residents. There is Alexis who won't go out in the sun just in case she gets too black and then everyone will think she is an African, Rosie from St Lucia starts dating one of the staff, and so he's sacked and she's moved out. Charlene stays out all night clubbing, turns up for breakfast and goes to bed until the evening, then climbs out the window to go clubbing again. Felicity comes to visit us every weekend from her family; she rocks in her chair all day long, and has visions of dragons and dinosaurs who are coming to gobble her up.

At mealtimes we join the younger ones. Samuel is eight years old and I can see his cat living inside his body. When he sits to eat, his cat sometimes jumps out of his body, and Samuel turns the table upside down and says he's not eating this shit. Nobody says anything because we know he's right; we all have to eat meals that have been kept in a hot plate for hours on end. Other times he jumps all over our table, picking the food from our plates and stuffing it into his mouth. When he manages to escape from his floor and gobbles up the fish from our aquarium in reception, the staff give up on him and send him off to a psychiatric unit called the End.

I settle in very quickly. Alexis teaches me how to behave black. I learn to swap my t's for d's, and start saying deres, dese, dat and dem. She teaches me how to say bloodclart and rasclart, and suck my teeth. I learn how to tie a headscarf on my head like Ena Sharples and turn my socks down to the right length. Alexis also teaches me how to dance to soul and reggae, and how to "crutch". She lifts up her floral gypsy skirt and lacy petticoat, takes a cushion off the settee and stuffs it between her legs and begins to walk around the playroom, saying: "See, it's simple. All black girls can crutch. Once you can do this, you can have anything you want."

Blessed is admitted a week after me. She arrives with a pink iron mark on her arm. She adopts me as her baby sister and we walk the streets together every weekend. Her Ghanaian mother turns up every other day and throws water and rice in the reception area, recites verses from the Bible, and then demands the return of her daughter. The staff try to calm her down while I and some other residents hide Blessed in the car park.

Blessed is in love with a man called Styx. When he visits, all the girls run into the reception to admire the diamond fixed onto his tooth, his leopard-skin jacket, silk shirt, farrahs, and croc shoes. He gives her money and we get to see the latest films like *King Kong* at the cinema. She takes me to his house and we listen to Rub A Dub on his sound system while he toasts lyrics to Irie tunes. He gives us Babycham to drink and we get very merry.

But one day an older version of Styx bursts in, brandishing a shotgun. He points it at Blessed, then at me and says: "One of you, out."

Blessed pushes me out and says: "I'm the oldest."

He follows me outside and makes me stand by the closed door, holding the gun to my head, and says: "One move and you're dead." Just as I try to leave my body, I hear a scream and then a crash. I turn my head and the gun butts it back. I hear a struggle, and then it goes all quiet. My voice is trapped inside my head. I'm too scared to leave my body because if I do, I know I won't be able to keep my cat out. I numb out so much that I can't even feel my cat scratching at my shoulder. Styx opens the door and says: "Let her go." Cursing, he hands him the gun and Styx points to Blessed huddled up on a makeshift double bed. He enters the room and shuts the door. I hear the floor thumping and Blessed's muffled sobs.

When the door opens next time, Blessed appears. Her Afro looks like a scarecrow and her make-up is graffitied all over her face. She avoids my questioning eyes and says: "I think we better leave." Styx pushes us out and we walk home in silence. It's the last time we see him. A month later Blessed is dragged back home screaming all the way to her mother's. Her case conference decides that there is not enough evidence that her mother caused the iron burn on her arm.

I decide to go on hunger strike after Blessed leaves. I've been here four months and it's Easter already. So I refuse to eat until the court case with Wunmi and my social workers comes up. When I don't eat my breakfast, Roger sends me to the deputy head's office for a chat. As soon as I get into Mr Harrington's office he begins to fidget in his chair. I stand by the door and he tells me to stop attention-seeking. I walk out, slam the door and scream: "Keep that pervert away from me."

I bump into Alexis in the corridor and she takes me to her room. She makes me sit while I watch her eat two big Cadbury easter eggs and half a box of Milk Tray. I miss dinner and she splits on me that I ate some chocolates in her room. So my hunger strike is over by teatime.

I slash my wrists the morning I have to go to court.

"Attention-seeking again," Mr Harrington says, bouncing up and down.

"I think she's serious," counters Roger.

They argue about whether they should call an ambulance. Meanwhile, I'm getting through all the bog roll and bravely stating: "If I run out of blood, that's all right."

The day nurse is buzzed and she does a good job at stopping my blood. Annabel, my cat and me all make it to court.

When I enter the room, Wunmi is standing on the other side. My year mistress, Mrs Squires, sits on one side and a social worker sits on the other. I can't resist a look at Wunmi; she catches my gaze, zips my lips with her eyes and locks my jaw. Mrs Squires reads out a catalogue of bruises recorded by the school over the past eighteen months. When Wunmi steps up to give her side of the story, I fly out of my body onto the ceiling and watch her pierce Mrs Squires with her eyes. Wunmi catches her gaze and a thin black cord leaps from her forehead, landing on Mrs Squires's shoulder. She trembles and I know a cat has jumped her body. I'm so scared that I fly back into my body.

Wunmi falls to the floor holding a Bible in her hand. She gyrates and raises her torso with her arms in the air, crying: "Lord, have mercy upon me. What have I done to deserve this evil day?"

Two official-looking people rush to pull Wunmi to her feet. She gesticulates and breaks down into tongues. As the two men manage to drag her to a seat, she turns towards me, catches her breath and says: "I know who you are." She takes hold of my gaze, and the African chief I've seen so many times in my dreams flashes between us and I feel a thump in my guts. Wunmi looks like a pile of gold one moment and a pile of ivory tusks the next. A bright light flashes between Wunmi and me and I can feel something taking over my body. I think it is my cat now living inside me, but when I look up at Mrs Squires, I can see my cat inside her. I pass out.

"Do you understand what has happened? You're under our care now. Section two. Your mother can never have you back. We just have to decide where you go to live next," is what I hear when I pull through.

I ignore him. I walk out of the court building straight into the beaming headlamps from cars leaving the car park. He pulls me back, stopping me from being run over by a police car. I feel as if I am possessed. That God is punishing me for all the evil deeds I've committed since I've been alive.

I stop in the middle of the car park, not able to move. Annabel appears and whispers: "What's wrong, Pauline? God has answered your prayers." My head starts to mutter and I know this thing inside me doesn't like the sound of God. The taunts becomes so loud that it manages to frighten Annabel away while I stay standing with cars honking at me to move out of the way. I can't recognise myself and wish I had given my body up to my cat. Something is living inside my body. I feel as if Wunmi is still controlling me, even though I don't have to see her anymore. My social worker pulls me into his car and says, don't worry, you'll feel a lot better in a day or two. The muttering in my head manages to drown out all my thoughts of God and Annabel, and I'm sick all the way back to the home.

Back at home, I insist the staff leave me alone. I run up to my bedroom and collapse on the floor. My head is heavy and feels like it is going to drop off. I know my cat has gone, but I have something constantly ringing in my head. It has such a shrill hiss that I call her Snake. Sometimes Snake travels down through my body, knocking me off my feet. Other times Snake coils herself around my body from head to toe. The buzzing in my body is like a force which pushes me in front of cars, makes me absent-minded and clumsy. I begin to crave for food, clothes, anything that will make the noise of Snake go away. When I can feel Snake inside me I sometimes think of being dead. But it's a different feeling from wanting to go and live in heaven with Annabel; it feels like I never want to move or breathe again. This heavy feeling makes me hang my head so low and walk with my body tensed and hands clenched. Sometimes people come up to me and say: "Cheer up, lovey. It may never happen." I scowl and walk away.

27

My Snake wakes me up. I know that there must be something else in the room because I feel sick and as if there's something gnawing at my gut. At the end of one of the spare beds are two balls of fur. I look again and see that someone has been admitted in the middle of the night. I switch the light on and the cats disappear. A girl with very red eyes emerges from Blessed's old bed.

"What are you in for?"

"Running away."

"From where?"

"Home."

"Why?"

The two balls of light-brown fur appear on her shoulders and she breaks down and cries. The night nurse pokes her head around the door and says: "Shush, what's all the noise about? It's 3am; get to sleep."

"Get a life. You're the one keeping everyone awake," I shout. She turns the light off and says: "Any more from you, young lady, and you're out." She shuts the door and leaves us alone.

"Is everyone like that here?" the new girl asks.

"Ignore the night staff; they think they're God. So how

comes you've run away from home?"

"I hate my aunt. She's stinking rich. Not like my mum and dad."

"So what happened to them?"

"My dad pissed off years ago – and my mum, well, she's…"

She pauses, and I can see her cats' hairs standing on end. And I know her mum is dead. Before I can change the subject, she spits out, "She was pushed."

"Pushed! How?"

"My stepdad got mad and pushed her through a window."

"Wow."

"And the police came that same night and took me and my brother to live with our mum's sister and brother-in-law. They despise the earth we walk on."

"Why?"

"My mum married a Gentile."

"What's that?"

"Someone who's not a Jew."

"My Uncle Boris was a Jew."

"But you're black."

"Watch out. Your cats."

"Shit, don't tell me there's fleas in this pit. I'm allergic to cats."

I roll about laughing. "Not that kind of cat, silly. There's someone who wants to borrow your body."

"My aunt's right about one thing. It's true that people who live in orphanages are all screwy."

The night nurse slings the door open again, turns the light on, and we both dive under our covers and pretend that we're fast asleep.

In the morning the new girl jumps up as if she's seen a

ghost and screams: "Where am I?" She doesn't recognise me and I can see that both her cats are living in her body. She has a fit, throws all the bed linen around and threatens to jump out of the window. I ignore her, get dressed, run downstairs to breakfast and tell one of the staff: "Get that nutter out of my room."

"Who, Sherry? She's an angel, I admitted her last night," says Roger with a smile. "She made me miss last orders down at the pub again, just like when you arrived."

"Well, you share a room with her then. I want her out by the time I get back from school."

Sherry's still in my room when I get back. She smiles, pouts her ruby lipstick lips and says: "Sorry about this morning. It just happens."

"Excuse me?"

"I just lose it sometimes."

"It's your two Siamese cats."

She trembles and the hair on her head begins to stick up. I flee the room. When I come up to bed, she's sitting on the floor smiling and apologises to me again. I don't mention her cats, I just smile back and say it's all right, I understand.

A week later Rita joins us in our room. She's a teddy girl, religiously ties her sandy-coloured hair back in a ponytail, wears a circle skirt and winkle-picker high-heeled shoes. I bump into her talking to one of her mates on the telephone: "Yevva ges, Mavva gan, Ivva gits, Grevva gate. Havva gere." I interrupt to insist that she tells me what she's saying. She sticks her face right in front of mine and says: "Yes, man, it's great here." Then she turns away, pushes some money into the phone, and speaks so fast that it sounds like gobbledy-gook.

When she puts the phone down, I beg her to teach me how to speak like her. "What's it worth?" she asks.

"Missing out on the new girl's introductory initiation to the children's home."

"And what's that?"

"Head flushed down the bog."

"Ivva gits, Avva ga, Davva geal."

"What's that you're saying?"

"It's a deal." And she flounces off up the corridor. Later that night, I hold her to our deal. She teaches Sherry and me to speak Pig Latin on the proviso she doesn't get flushed. The night nurse comes in and gives us a warning, and she tells her to "Fuvva guck, Ovva gof."

Sherry and I crack up laughing, as we know exactly what she has said.

"One more warning and I'll report the lot of you to the boss." She slams our door shut.

"How do I say my name?" Sherry demands.

"Shavva git, Tavva gi, Pavva gants."

I crack up again, doing my hardest to muffle my laughter under the sheets. "What, what?" asks Sherry.

"I've worked it out. She says your name is Shitty Pants." Sherry's hair sticks up and her two cats jerk her about. "Duck!" I shout. Rita and I lie prostrate on our beds and listen to a lamp and a chair crashing against the wall.

"For fuck sake, it was a joke," says Rita.

"There are no jokes in this room. You better keep to the deal," I reply. In a week we're both stuttering away in the lingo. We drive the staff mad by refusing to speak in proper English and in three weeks all the kids and the members of staff on the adolescent unit are joining in.

More kids have passed through the assessment centre than I've brushed my teeth. And I'm grateful that I've got two mates who stay longer than one month. Rita and Sherry have been chucked out of their schools and get to do education in the home, which finishes well before proper school times. They hang out in the local parks most afternoons and I do my utmost to get suspended from Edgware Towers so I can have the soft option of attending school in the home. But most times one of the staff spends an hour on the phone to my year mistress begging her to take me back. I demand to see the boss in the home, and tell him that he doesn't understand how hard it is to go to school when your mates are having much better fun in the education unit.

"You've got a brain, use it for a change, instead of following people who will only lead you down the wrong path," says Mr Martin.

"It's not fair."

"There are many things in life which aren't fair, now get to school before I send you to the End along with Samuel."

Everyone is scared of being sent there as it's rumoured to be worse than Alcatraz, so I do as I am told, and attempt to stay at Edgware Towers.

28

Sherry has a wobbler in the morning. The breakfast toast is as stiff as cardboard, and you know that Maud the cook has grilled it at 5am and put it on the hot plate for us to eat two and half hours later. Sherry takes a bite, slings it across the dining hall like a Frisbee, and then looks at a new girl sitting at the next table. "Get her out!"

I can see one of her cats and that's a warning to tell me she is about to erupt. Cutlery and plates go flying and most of us freeze until she has nothing left to throw. The staff have learnt that she's best left alone until she calms down. Sherry winks at Rita and me and says: "Cavva gon, Favva ge, Ravva gence, Ivva gin, Avva gour, Ravva goom, Navva gow." We leave the table and run upstairs for a conference in our room.

Sherry's cats make her froth at the mouth. Rita and I have worked out that if one of us stands on her feet and the other holds her arms, she'll get back to normal quickly. So we take hold of her and wait for her to calm down so she can tell us what is wrong.

"That new bitch is my cousin. I want her out now."

Rita says: "She's in the room next door, I heard her being admitted in the middle of the night."

191

"Later," Sherry adds, "when there aren't so many staff about, we'll get her."

When I get back from school, Rita grabs me and whispers, "Wait for us in the basement." Minutes later the cousin is frog-marched into the bogs and we're shoving her head down the toilet pan, giving it a long, hard flush.

"If you don't leave, it will get worse," Sherry warns.

She grasses all three of us up to the staff and we're barred from going out at night for a week. After our first night of being gated, the three of us make a dash for the front doors after tea and decide not to return. We walk around until it gets dark. Sherry begins to take a turn and complains about having frostbite. But none of us want to go back because of losing face. We end up climbing onto a college roof and huddling up together under two parkas and a crombie coat to keep us warm. I pray it doesn't rain.

"At least it's safer than sleeping on the streets," says Rita. "And we're doing this for you," she says to Sherry.

Sherry begins to sing "Twinkle, Twinkle little star" and before she can burst into full volume, Rita is down on her like a ton of bricks. "Cut it out, I want to sleep."

"Look, it's Annabel playing with her friends."

"Who?" both Rita and Sherry ask.

"Look in the sky." I point. "They used to be my friends."

"They're shooting stars. What are you on? Whatever it is give us some," says Sherry.

"I don't believe it! I'm lying in between two head cases," says Rita and curls her body around my back.

I realise tonight that I'm becoming too old for my confidante Annabel to live in my head and perhaps now I should start relying on my mates in the home to show me the ropes. I daren't tell them about Snake as they really would think I was mad. I fall asleep with gravel scratching on my face.

"I'm going home," Sherry says as soon as she wakes up. "Look, all my clothes are wet," and she begins to froth at the mouth. Rita and I look at each other, and know that we shouldn't take a chance. So we climb down off the roof and make our way home in time for breakfast. Nobody says much when we arrive back. We complete our week's punishment, Sherry's cousin is moved out, and things get back to normal.

School is becoming a real bore. Now that I'm not living with Wunmi, its appeal has gone. Henrietta's mother says she can't play with me anymore because I live in a children's home. And it's much more fun with my mates in the home than cheeking teachers with Josephine at school. But the staff are still down on me about my attendance level and remind me of Mr Martin's warning. So every day I try my hardest to make my way to school, but the continuous hissing in my head seems to hypnotise me and I find myself back on the bus, travelling to where Sherry and Rita will be hanging out in the afternoons.

When I arrive at their regular haunt in the park, they're sitting with a bunch of teenagers who are all nose-diving into crisp packets filled with Evo Stick glue. My friends frighten me when they all sniff the glue, but I want to be part of the gang. So I sit still most afternoons and watch, hoping they will forget to ask me if I want a sniff. Someone I don't know gets up and thinks he's Evil Kneevil. He jumps onto a racer and cycles straight into a tree, pick himself up, jumps back on and shouts out: "Watch me!" Nobody does; they just dig their noses deeper into their crisp packets. Rita thinks she's Bruce Lee's sister and threatens a kung fu fight with anyone who passes by and stares. Sherry sprints around the park shouting at full volume that she has survived. I watch most days as my mates go doollaley on glue. I get high on saying no, and from a distance I can inhale enough to put my Snake to sleep. I'm able to sit calmly and pass as one of the gang.

I'm always agitated after a session out with the gang. One of the boys has broken his arm and another fell out of a tree while he was swinging from branch to branch like a monkey. And Rita thought she could fly until she knocked herself out by diving head-first off a climbing frame into a bed of roses. Sherry cuts herself with a razor blade and offers her blood to the true Messiah.

I buy pills from the chemist and threaten every day to take them if Rita and Sherry don't stop. Today my Snake takes a grip of me in the park. She wants me to sniff. I panic, my stomach begins to gurgle and hiss so loud that Sherry thinks she is having the best ever trip. I seize her crisp packet and my nose is instantly snorting on the fumes of the glue. I fall off the park bench and start rolling around all over the grass. Everyone stops sniffing. I look up and it's like my Snake has eight beady eyes peering down on top of me.

"Is she all right?" I hear one of the boys ask.

I giggle, and Rita says: "Yeah, our Pauline's okay." They all go back to their crisp packets and don't notice me leaving as I wriggle along the grass.

Snake has a hold of me, her hiss is so loud that I lose all sense of direction and don't know how I manage to stumble home. When I bump into a member of staff, I use the excuse that I'm feeling sick and have taken the afternoon off school. I put myself to bed and frantically pray for God's or Annabel's help. My body is heavy and I fall into a fitful stupor, with Snake twisting and gyrating my body.

I wake up to Sherry screaming the home down. A new member of staff, called Imogen, with tattoos slinking down both arms, comes running into our bedroom, takes hold of Sherry and starts screaming too. Rita, half sober, says; "No, not her. It's Pauline who's taken the pills." I can see Sherry waving empty boxes in my face.

Imogen takes them from her and says to me: "Pauline, you wouldn't do a thing like this. I was told you were the sensible one."

I roll over, and Sherry and Rita, still high on glue, jump up and down on my bed, telling Imogen to do something. I'm wondering what all the fuss is about. Rita and Sherry pull me up and my body is like jelly. My legs give way as I try to stand. Sherry tries shoving her fingers down my throat, but Rita says: "No, let's take her downstairs." Between the two of them, they prop me up and slide me down the stairs. My head is full of ambulance noises and Snake. The next thing I know I have a tube rammed down my throat and I am emptied inside out.

I lie in bed staring at the hospital ceiling. Annabel appears and before I can thank her, she is preaching: "God is your saviour, Pauline. You must..." But Snake cuts her off mid-sentence and all I can see now are flashing lights above me. I give in, letting Snake take over my whole body and mind. My fretful dreams tell me that Snake is a Spirit who is angry at the world. She was flogged to death working as a slave in a plantation field. Since then she has been trying to be reborn for hundreds of years, but Snake is so angry that she is stillborn every time. I don't care that she borrows my body. Although Annabel is still my friend, I've lost my faith in God and I am ready to die.

The head of the home comes to visit me the next day and

says: "What are you?" He hesitates, "A twit." I give a half smile, knowing I have no strength to beat him to the punch line today. He lectures me about taking glue, says I'm mixing in the wrong company, and that it's time he found me a new home.

When I arrive home two days later, Sherry is packing her bags. In her case conference last week, it was decided that she'd be sent to the End. She's been acting up ever since as it's the worst place to go. Samuel's there and when he escapes he turns up in the reception area doped up to the eyeballs from all the drugs they inject. The police come and cart him off, with him kicking and screaming to stay with us in the home. Sherry is dragged out by four members of staff. She has sworn Rita and me to an oath that we'll help her to escape. Rita leaves a week later, she's sent off to some crusty foster parents all the way in Catford. They're in their sixties, shop in the Co-op and have Tupperware parties every Sunday afternoon. I'm left on my own with two empty beds, waiting to find out who will turn up next in the middle of the night.

29

When all three of us meet at Paddington station to live on the run, Sherry's arms are black and blue from all the restraints and injections used to sedate her at the End. She spends the first day slurring her words with her two cats sleeping peacefully on her shoulder while Rita and I suss out a place to make our home.

We sleep in parks and make friends with the local drunks. It's wet and cold most of the time, and Sherry keeps on threatening to go back to the End. Rita reckons if we give ourselves up, we'll be sent to the End too. So we all agree to continue roughing it, and think of ways to earn some dosh. We cash in on bonfire night by stuffing a Guy Fawkes and making badges that read "Help the Aged". We troop down to Paddington station, rattle our tins and chant: "Help us to help the aged."

"Shavva git," I say.

"What's wrong?" Rita asks.

In Pig Latin I say, "See that woman coming towards us, she used to work in the home."

And before we can think of an escape plan, she's in our faces: "Afternoon, Pauline," she grins. "Collecting for the elderly, are you?"

"None of your business," says Sherry.

"Sherry, shut it," I say and nod my head, wondering what to do next.

"Well, if the police stop you, tell them you're taking it to St Marks Old People's Home down the road." She slips a fiver in the tin and walks off.

"Phew, that was close," says Rita.

"Yeah, she's cool."

"Shame you weren't so bloody cool when you first clapped eyes on her," Sherry snaps back.

"Who rattled your cage? Leave it out, Sherry and let's make some cash," Rita barks back.

We collect £10 that day. It stops us from arguing over what we're going to eat and we pitch for a covered doorway to sleep in that night. Sherry wants us all to relocate to a squat she knows. But the last Rita heard, three girls were raped, so we're staying put.

On our third day of shaking tins for the aged, the Sweeney arrive dressed in blue. "Are you Pauline Charles, Rita Jones and Sherry Brooks?"

I make a run for it, but Sherry and Rita happily give themselves up. I jump on the first bus I see and get off in the West End. I walk around and spend my money in the amusement arcades, and make friends with a wilting lady waiting on a street corner. Every time she blinks she reveals a deep gash running diagonally over one of her eyelids. "Not got a home to go to. You're too young for the streets. Make yourself useful. What's your name?"

"Pauline."

She looks at me as if I'm crazy. "You're new on the streets, I can tell. That sounds like your real name to me. Gotta make one up when you're in these parts of town. I'm Brandy. Stand here. If you see a traffic warden, or a big black guy arriving in a Mercedes, come and bang on my Mini."

"Who's Mercedes?"

"Wisening up already. That's a great name for him. Mercedes, I like that. Don't worry, you'll recognise him all right. He'll turn up in a big black car with dark windows. As soon as you hear him just bang on this Mini over here."

She walks off and I stand on the corner eating chips. Every fifteen minutes a different man comes up to me and says: "You seen Brandy?" I just point to her car and my eyes dart around looking for Mercedes. He never arrives, and I end up sleeping with Brandy in her Mini, which she moves to an alleyway nearby.

In the morning she takes me to a café and feeds me egg and bacon on toast and then asks: "So what are you going to do with yourself today? Don't look at me. You can't hang out with me all day. Go home, it's gotta be better than here."

"I don't want to go home."

A black man appears at the doorway of the greasy café, wearing a sovereign on every finger, a gold chopper eater round each wrist, and a gold chain as thick as rope noosed around his neck. He smiles and it looks like gold is falling out of his mouth. Brandy digs me in the ribs, pushes a tenner in my hand and whispers "Run!" Before I can get up he's over at our table and grabbing her bleached hair, demanding: "Where's the breds?" He slaps her in the face, takes the purse from the table and empties out all the money. Then he turns to me and says: "And who's this new little virgin?"

"Leave her alone," Brandy shouts and kicks me in the shins. I get the hint and leg it to a bus stop which I know will take me all the way back to the home. I don't care if they send me to the End, at least I'll be with Sherry. Two weeks of living on the run is not as glamorous as the stories I've heard from some of the older girls in the home.

Everyone is relieved when I return home, but the staff say I've changed. I know it's true because Snake has made me so absent-minded that I've even started to get low grades at school when I turn up. And my moods tick around the clock every hour.

I keep in touch with Rita and Sherry by letter and telephone, and I don't care much for the new people who arrive and leave the home a few weeks later. I want to be with my old friends. I become a loner, keeping myself to myself.

"It's time for you to move on," says Roger one day while I'm sitting destroying all the table tennis bats in the games room, picking off the rubber and the foam and flicking it at anybody I don't like. "You've been here over a year, it's almost Christmas again. That's far too long. Kids should only be here six weeks and then moved on."

I ignore him and throw the bats about before going up to my room. A few days later, a decision is made at my case conference to send me back to the Village where I grew up. I'm not happy with the decision but Snake is never happy with anything she's offered. My face is hot and I feel my heart jump; Annabel has come alive. She invades my head, and tells me this is great. She's very happy about going back to the Village and I know she is trying to make up with me.

30

I'm a London girl when I move back to the Village. I talk about red, gold and green, and chant Jah Rasta Fari everywhere I go. I hardly recognise anyone in the Village and many of the Cottages have been closed down. Most of us live on the kinder green, and the family I left behind have been fostered out, or have grown up and are living out in the big world. My old friends Pedro and Terry think I'm off my rocker. They don't have much time for me. My new Uncle and Aunty are scared I'll turn the other coloured children against them, because I correct them and tell them we're not coloured, we're black, and that they're racist if they don't agree. They say I'm trying to start a Black Panther movement, and I get moved into the Cottage with all the children who are labelled troublesome.

I don't care as most of the black kids in the Village are living in Revelations Cottage, which we all nickname "The Siege". Nobody calls my new house parent Uncle Ron. We call him Hitler and everyone hates his guts. His wife walks around as if she is his ghost and shakes every time one of us black kids passes her in the corridor. Most of us go a.w.o.l and ignore the ten o'clock curfew. I learn to shimmy up and down the drainpipes and stay out as long as I like. I make friends with the next-door neighbours, Leila and Sadie, who've both had a stint of living in London. Sadie is quite new to the Village and Leila has returned, like me, after communication broke down with her mum.

Sadie and I go to the same school. She's black and her mum is from British Guyana. She wears long beaded braids which clatter when she moves and has a smile which sets everyone off into laughter. We're called the swots because we're the only ones from the Village who attend the local grammar school. I have to do Latin with Mrs Braze, who gives me the hiccups when teaching me hic, haec, hoc. My music teacher is found at least once a week slumped outside the school gates drunk, and my favourite teacher, Mr Ford, is sacked for being caught stealing art books from a shop in town. The geography teacher makes a point of telling the whole class every week that people in Africa and India defecate and expectorate on the streets.

The deputy headmistress stops all of us most days outside the school, checking to see that her girls are still wearing their ties at home time: "This is a respectable school, please keep your tie inside your jumper." She points to my skirt, and says: "It's far too long. And pull those ridiculous socks up, before I pack you off to kindergarten."

Sadie and I are the only black girls in the school and at dinnertime some of the girls ask if we can talk like real coloured people. "Go on, let's hear you talk Jamaica," one of Sadie's classmates asks.

We show off and step into our starring roles most lunchtimes. When we meet in the dinner hall I mimic a "rude boys" walk by limping rhythmically along the floor and come out with: "Long time no see. Ya all right, Dready?"

"Yes man. So wa appen," Sadie replies and slaps me on my hand.

"Jah Rasta Fari."

We get a clap and go our separate ways as we both know there's not much more we know how to say in a Jamaican accent. If we bump into each other in the dinner queue, Sadie says: "I suppose we can talk Jamaican anyway."

"Yeah, but they don't know that," and I give her five, and say: "Bomber Seed."

The girls crowd again and ask us to keep on talking Jamaica.

"Later will be greater," I say.

Sadie translates: "She means you have to wait until tomorrow." And then we go our separate ways again, joining our friends at the dinner table and blending back in with our white school friends.

Sadie introduces Leila and me to Lady Esquire. It comes in a small bottle, is transparent and conditions shoes. After school some days we hide out in the bedroom with a bed rammed up against the door. Sadie pours some of the fluid on a cloth and sniffs and Leila and I do the same. It blows us away, and before we know it we're all rolling about the floor. I like it because it puts Snake to sleep. Instead of the constant call in my head I can hear sounds ding-donging there instead. Traffic lights flash in front of my eyes and I have to hopscotch in between them to try and save my life. Or I often get stuck in the same maze and have to find my way out. It's like I have a game of space invaders programmed in my brain. After half an hour I begin to feel groggy and can hear Snake waking up. When the bottle is empty and we're all looking for some more Sadie always says; "I suppose we're smashed anyway." We laugh and start meeting up more and more until we're not making our way to school.

Instead we meet up with James, a white friend of Sadie's who is triple our age, with grey hair and a beard. We head out to the forest and sniff all day. We go shopping for our Lady Esquire, filling our bags with plenty of bottles and anything else we can lay our hands on. I'm banned from Sadie and Leila's Cottage as their Aunty and Uncle, Mr and Mrs Stephens, complain that I'm a bad influence. "You're from the problem Cottage next door, leave my kids alone. They were as good as gold before you came along," says their Aunty Millie, when we're all found out truanting from school.

Leila and I soon get fed up with hanging out with Sadie and James. Sadie says she's in love and wants to be with him on her own, and so we begin to entertain ourselves. We return to our schools, but at home time Leila and I meet up to raid the local shops. Every time I steal it gives me a good feeling and makes the hiss in my head disappear. I know it's wrong and I can sometimes hear my old Aunty Claire say: "Thou shalt not steal," but I don't care anymore. The excitement I get from being invisible in shops makes me want to do it even more. Leila never talks about stealing being wrong. She thinks that because we live in an orphanage we have a right to help ourselves to anything we want.

Sadie bumps into us one day on her way to meeting James. "I suppose you are walking normally," she says.

"Of course we are man, check this," and I do my black stylee walk.

"'Tis normal," she insists.

And the next moment Leila drops a box from between her thighs.

"I suppose it is normal to have an iron sandwiched between your legs."

"What's your problem?" I say.

"Come on, Pauline, you may as well show Sadie what you've got too."

I take out a heavyweight steel frying pan.

"I suppose you do need all this." Sadie picks up Leila's box and tries walking with it between her legs. She laughs and asks when we're going nicking again.

Leila and I begin to take orders from our friends in the home and at school. In the evenings I'm smuggled into her Cottage, and we run a market stall from the playroom. All the Village kids come and buy jeans and tops, or make orders for our next shopping spree. Sadie keeps a lookout for their house parents, and warns us if they're about to walk down the hallway.

The local high street begins to complain about the Village kids stealing from their shops. So our house parents do a raid on everybody's room over the age of eleven. Everything that is stacked up under mine and Leila's bed and piled into our wardrobe is taken back, along with Sadie's and a few others who are hiding stolen goods. All of us who've been caught are banned from walking down the high street, and our pocket money is stopped for one week. So we move the market stall to Terry's backyard shed as nobody will suspect her of being up to no good.

My house parents start trying to ground me every night, so on Fridays I don't come home from school. I meet up with Leila and go home to her mum's for the weekend.

31

Leila's mum is white and claims she was born under the Cockney Bow bells. However, Leila reckons her grandma gave her up for charity and dumped her there out of good will. Leila's mum has six kids. The oldest has a Jamaican dad and was thrown out as soon as she turned thirteen. The two youngest have different white dads and have been adopted together in Kent. Her mum doesn't talk about the others, except for Leila's dad, whose supposed to be an Italian GI from America and who Leila's never met. Leila disagrees and tells everybody her dad is a Bagan, and that's why she's got frizzy hair and tanning skin. Leila demanded she be put in a home at the age of twelve.

Her mum smokes over fifty a day and swigs from a bottle of brandy as if it's her mother's nipple. She lives on a street where some of the houses are derelict, and the others are sinking or tumbling down. Her front room is filled with black men every evening from the local betting shop. They play dominoes all night, gambling away their winnings. Her live-in man, Sir Judge, plays tamla motown, ska, dub and calypso in the front room, attracting all the Bagans and Trinis from all over London to his shabeen every Saturday night.

The walls are decorated with West Indian Hot Pepper

Sauce, streaks of Guinness Punch, dumpling stew, and flaking paint. And Leila's mum is lucky if she escapes the casualty unit before the end of a weekend. Her nose looks like it belongs to an African and she walks about the house in sunglasses, talking to herself about the day when she'll get to visit the Windies. She's been well trained and can make the best ackee and salt fish, dumplings, curried mutton, and rum punch in the East End.

When we arrive home for the weekend on Friday nights, Leila knocks the door very hard. "Uw the ell is that?" her mum asks.

"Me."

"Fuck off out of 'ere. You chose to live in a 'ome. Let them look after ya."

"Oh come on, Mum, open up."

She opens the door and says: "Look what the cat's dragged in," while looking at me.

"Mum, Pauline's with me."

"No, she ain't staying 'ere," and tries to push the door shut. Leila's foot is wedged in its way and she pulls out all the meat we've nicked from her Cottage freezer. Her mum takes the joint of beef, the mincemeat and chicken, and then tries again to shut the door on Leila's foot.

I pull out a bottle of brandy that I've crutched from the local off licence. Leila grabs it out of my hand and pushes it round the door, calling out to her mum again. She tries to take it but Leila snatches it back and says: "Pauline's staying with me."

Her mum gives in, but before our feet are pinning down the dodgy floorboards in the hallway, she shouts at me: "None of your bloody nonsense. The Stephens 'ave said you're a bad influence on our Leila. I shouldn't be lettin' you stay."

Leila pushes past her mum and I follow upstairs into her room. She unlocks the padlock and once we're inside, we bolt ourselves in. It's paradise. We've carpeted it wall to wall, put together a four poster bed, and covered the walls with velvet wallpaper from all the money we've made selling clothes. Her mum bangs on the door and tells us to unlock it. But we ignore her, turn on our new record player and listen to the latest records we've stolen from the shops, and plan what we're going to wear from the clothes we've nicked earlier that week.

We wear our brand new Hawaiian shirts, carpenter trousers and silver plastic sandals. Leila tries out colouring my hair. I can feel the dye burning my scalp and she shouts "Shit!"

"What?"

"I'm really sorry."

"Let me see the mirror."

"No."

We fight and I manage to push her out of the way to get to the mirror tiles we've fitted onto the wall. I look like a pint of Guinness gone off. I'm blonde at the front and by the time you get to the back my hair is ginger.

"Where's the crazy colour?"

"Oh shit, I forgot to bring it."

We fight again until Leila takes the green dye out of her bag. My hair starts off as bright green at the front and by the time you get to the back it's blue. We both decide it looks cool and put on our bandit glasses to polish off our outfits. We unlock the door and march downstairs into the slum. Leila's mum says "Jesus Christ" and looks at me.

"He hasn't risen yet," I retort back.

"You sure, luv?"

"It's okay, Mum, you've got the DTs," says Leila.

"Enough of your fuckin' cheek. Brass, otherwise you're not going out." Leila chucks her a fiver. She picks it up, stuffs it in her bra, and then starts on me.

"Where's your bloody mum?"

"I haven't got one."

"'Aven't got one? Well, why don't you find someone else's mum to sponge off, and leave me and my daughter alone."

"Mum, you've got your money."

"Leila! She's not to come back tonight."

I take a fiver out of my sock, and thrust it in her face.

"Okay, just this once."

Leila and I are used to the same drama every time we visit at weekends. We plead with Sir Judge to give us a lift into town. But he's having none of it so we catch two buses all the way to the nightclub. Leila gets jittery on the bus, "How old am I?"

"Eighteen."

"Yeah, but what year was I born in?"

"1960."

"What are you going to say?"

"Twenty-seventh of the eleventh, 1961."

"How comes you always remember?"

"I don't. I just work it out every time we're going out."

The bus pulls into Trafalgar Square, we jump off and stop the first two white guys dressed as soul heads we see heading towards Global. We ask if we can be their girlfriends until we get into the club, as the bouncers are particular about the black people they let in. When we arrive at the queue we bump into Sadie, Pedro and Terry from the Village, who are well sick they don't look as good as us. We know we're the business, we're never seen twice in any outfit, and we look so groovy that we become the talk of the club.

Leila gets her date of birth right when our turn comes to be let inside and the bouncers don't bat an eyelid at us as we drape ourselves around our white boyfriends' bodies. Once we're in we're off, and spend half the night running away from the two guys who helped us to get in. Sadie and the others don't get in. The club has let in its quota of black people, so the bouncers use the excuse that they don't look eighteen. They join the rest of the black people who've been refused entry. Half an hour later, some clubbers open the fire exit doors and all the blacks come running in.

Soul is played on the ground floor, funk in the middle and jazz right at the top. I can dance so well now that I often pull a crowd, and I get drunk from twisting and spinning my body around on the dance floor. The more I dance, the more Snake comes alive, and it is the place where Snake and I seem to play. Snake is fearless, she whips me into a frenzy and I can do somersaults and acrobats in the air. I can spin for sixty seconds on one foot, then spin for another thirty on my hands, ending up swinging my legs around, my arms supporting me on the floor, while Leila flicks herself over me. Leila and I become known as the best girl dancers in town. We drink jungle juice, black currant and lemonade, and say no to all the speed, black bombers, and blues being passed around. I've been scared off pills since the day Snake took over my body in the hospital bed. Every time I hear her hiss it reminds me of her death. She whips me so hard inside that I sometimes feel it was me who died in the plantation fields. But when I dance, Snake puts me in a trance and I feel that my body is invincible, and nothing can make me die.

At 3am we're all pushed out onto the streets and everyone walks to Trafalgar Square to catch a night bus home. I'm fourteen again and Leila is fifteen as we try to prove our real ages to the bus conductor on the way home.

Sir Judge grabs Leila when we arrive back at the house. But she pushes him off and he pulls her mum instead, winding her and grinding her to the ground to the sound of a needle jumping all over his calypso tune. It's quiet in their home tonight, the sound of men slamming dominoes doesn't knock the pictures off our bedroom wall while we're trying to sleep.

32

By the time I reach fourteen I'm famous. My picture is in the local newspaper. When I turn up at school, a friend says that she didn't know I was looking for a mum and dad. I abscond from school after that; I tell my social worker I don't want no stupid family and if the Village wants to get rid of me, I'm quite happy looking after myself. My house parents have been locking me out most nights, bolting all the doors and windows, so I've been sleeping in the shed when Leila and Sadie aren't able to sneak me into their Cottage next door.

I meet back up with Sherry and start living on the run. We live in squats and shoplift all day. When the police pick me up no home will take me because I'm so bad; eventually I'm packed off to the Lodge, a lock-up for young people who run away and are in trouble with the police. I've been arrested for loitering with intent to steal.

When I arrive outside a big white house, surrounded by a tall fence of barbed wire, Annabel surprises me with a visit. She hovers above my head and makes my face feel warm. She whispers: "I told you so." I ignore her and look down at my feet and see a caterpillar crawling along the ground. I know it's Annabel trying to reach out to me, I can hear her whispering: "Friends forever" just like the days we used to sit and play beside the sandpit in the Village. I stamp on it and my ears are screeching with Snake's call. Annabel turns into a yellow butterfly and brushes my forehead goodbye. I try to catch her, but she's off up in the skies. Snake strangles my tears by coiling up in my throat and I'm distracted by the sound of female voices shouting aloud. A car door slams shut and a social worker that I hardly know hands me a bag full of clothes. As soon as we enter the building, an alarm is set off and men and women come running from all directions. I'm rigid, clenched tight as I watch them drag a girl along the corridor while she shouts the house down.

My social worker abandons me. I'm left in a house where I can't even see the sunshine because the wooden slats on the windows block it out. I sit on my bed, staring at the other nine lived-in beds, wondering what to do next when one of my new dorm mates dressed in a T-shirt and jeans walks in. Her arms are razor-bladed from shoulder to hand, not even a pin can fit in between her scars. She wears them like trophies. She smiles, says: "Hi, my name is Meg. What's yours?" And I can't believe how happy she is with her arms looking like that. I flinch.

"New here?" I nod, and she says: "Well, you better fucking watch out, they're bastards in here."

I stay in my room for the first few days, only coming out for education and meals. But soon I'm one of the girls, insulting the staff and causing havoc wherever I go. By week two I've learnt how to pickpocket, open doors without a key and forge signatures on cheques.

At night times we're sentenced to silence from 9pm, and so we play double dare, true love, kiss or promise, and end up having to sing songs out loud when it's a dare. Meg has to sing "There's Ten in the Bed", and we all get to act it out. I get a dare next to sing "Ten Green Bottles Hanging On The

Wall", and the girls say it has to be even louder. Everyone joins in until our door opens and the deputy head, Mr Treener, stands in our dormitory. He walks up to my bed, glares with his green eyes and gives me a harsh warning. When he leaves my mates say: "Come on, tell us, what did he say?"

I pretend I'm asleep but Meg jumps all over me. I push her off and say quietly: "He said if I don't shut up, one black bottle will be locked up before I go to court." Everyone falls about laughing and Mr Treener marches back in, hauls me out of bed and takes me to his office.

He sits me down and says: "I can see you're not like most of the girls we get here. When are you going to learn?" I just sit, and shiver in his upright wooden chair. He bulges out of his black leatherette swivel chair, and talks to me about wars in the world, and all the starving children, and asks me what I think I can to do to help.

I say: "Tell Europe to take its big fat nose out of other people's affairs. And if you're worried about starving children, why don't you change jobs."

He looks at me and says: "You've got a brain, why don't you use it?"

"Yeah, like a hole in the head."

"Come on, Pauline, shake this behaviour off. Do you really want to spend the rest of your life locked up? There's not many like you who've got half your chance."

I can feel Snake not liking Mr Treener because my stomach starts to throb. I demand he gives me a dressing gown before I freeze my tits off. He laughs and I tell him to go fuck himself and push all his papers off his desk. Mr Treener presses the emergency alarm and three night staff come running in and ship me off to the padded cell for the night.

I fight with Snake tonight, we bounce from wall to wall, and I tell her that it's time she left and gave me back my body. But Snake just pushes me to the floor, leaving me with a more intense hiss in my head. I'm thrown around so much that I fall asleep exhausted in the middle of the floor. I'm unprepared for my appearance in court the next day.

My case is thrown out of court. I was arrested under the SUS laws – Suspect Under Suspicion – but there's not enough evidence so it's agreed that because I'm homeless and no one will accept me in their children's home I'll be sent to a hostel for young women aged over sixteen who've just left care.

I'm lucky as everyone said I would get borstal. And it's great as I can get up to whatever I want. But it soon turns out not to be so great: men climb through windows at night, women steal each other's belongings, and a fight breaks out every other hour.

After a week there, I decide it's far safer to move out and live back on the streets with Sherry. She teaches me all I need to know about how to survive on the streets. She walks into shops, picks up televisions and just walks straight back out. We walk the streets together all day, stand on the tube platforms during rush hour, push up against strangers and reach inside their breast pockets. We squeeze up behind women along Oxford Street and unzip or pop open their bags, dipping deep inside. I'm so excited with my new life. My body is always alert, and I no longer walk as if I'm in a bad mood. Snake is calm and I stop having thoughts of wanting to be dead.

When we make lots of money we pay to stay in a hotel and always go shopping the next day. We buy Burberry Macs, cashmere suits and silk blouses, and go out raving all night. We often bump into Leila in the nightclubs. Tonight she is decked out in a Muscat fur coat. "Right, that's it," says Sherry, "we're having furs tomorrow."

The next day we travel up to town with one of her boyfriends. "Here, hold our coats," Sherry orders, and he does what he is told, and waits patiently outside the department store while we go inside. "Where is the fur department?" Sherry demands. A courteous shop assistant directs us up the escalators to the second floor. "There they are," Sherry says with delight. She pushes the furs chained to the hangers along the rail and says: "Quick, here take this. Flick the chain like this. Quick, for heaven's sake."

Hey presto, the furs are released and we step inside them as if they've always been sleeping on our backs.

"Can I help you?" a shop assistant politely asks.

"Yes, we're looking for the mink range, do you have any?" Sherry charmingly inquires.

The assistant replies, speaking through her nose: "Yes, follow me," and leads us to the minks. She mirrors every step we take and stands behind us, breathing down our necks. I almost trip up as we follow.

"Stovva gop, Fuvva guck, Kuvva ging, Trevva gemb, Bluvva ging," Sherry is muttering under her breath – stop fucking trembling. I pull myself together, take a deep breath and say: "Oh, these are absolutely wonderful! What do you think, Sherry?"

She turns to the assistant and complains that they're the wrong bloody cut and colour for the wedding. "Is that all you've got?"

"Yes," replies the assistant, somewhat embarrassed.

She tries to interest us in a different range, but before she can convince us to have a look, Sherry is telling her, "Oh well, it will have to be Harrods, I'm sure they'll have what we're looking for." And waltzes out of the department store, leading me down the escalators looking as proud as a queen, our heads held high as if we own everything in the shop.

As we step onto the curb, my heart is pumping blood at the pace of a four-minute mile. Sherry smiles and says: "Now that's how you do it." She rescues our Burberrys from her gobsmacked bloke and hails a taxi to take us home.

Sherry starts spending all our money on heroine and cocaine and I get scared. I start hanging out with Leila again, who is back living at her mum's. She's sixteen now and decides it's better than the Village. I've completely abandoned school, but as long as I stay in touch with my social worker I get money to stay in bed and breakfast, and when they cut it, I sleep on friends' floors.

Leila and I travel up to Birmingham, Manchester and Leeds to go shoplifting and pick-pocketing for our keep. We take two empty shopping trolleys and come back with them filled to the brim with household goods and clothes. We get caught from time to time, but most of the time we charm our way out of it. Sometimes we spin the yarn about being poor little orphans from Dr Barnardo's. Other times Leila says her mum is an alcoholic and has drank away all her dad's money. If the store detectives are really heavy, we both break down in tears and say that our adopted mum is in hospital with a weak heart and if she knew we were stealing, it would kill her instantly.

But one day just as we board the train back home to London, plainclothes police pull us back and ask to look inside our trolleys. They pull out leather trousers, cashmere jumpers and designer-labelled goods, look at us and say: "You're under arrest." We follow them into an office on the platform and then we're taken off to the local police station for the night.

The next day Leila is seen in Birmingham Magistrates Court and released on bail. I have to stay another night until the social workers arrive. I'm fifteen, still a juvenile, and my court sends me off to the infamous Hole to wait for sentencing at Crown Court.

I step into a police van, handcuffed, and travel with one other young woman who was remanded that day. The windows are blacked out, and I try to imagine the route from Birmingham to London. We stare at the floor for two hours until the van stops and then we're ushered into the Hole. It smells of boiled cabbage, and looks as if it's overcast everyday. I'm strip-searched three times, and seen by the doctor, the counsellor and the minister within my first hour. I move into a cell with four wrought-iron bunks. I gain six mothers and one grandmother overnight. They all agree they don't want me to see or hear anything which might corrupt my mind. I'm spoilt so much that I feel like I've been sent on a summer camp. They stuff my ears with plugs so I can't hear anything at night, and there is always one of them at my side when I'm not on the education wing. I go to education during the day, and sleep as much as I can at night. An inmate passes on to me that Sherry is in borstal, she's just been put down for cheque book and card.

People move in and out of the cells every day, and the women like me who are waiting to be sentenced live on doses of Mogadon and Largactil to calm their nerves.

They enrol me up for a dose and teach me how to keep it under my tongue until I get back to the cells. I have to swallow a dose one day as the doctor tells me to open my mouth. That night Snake appears in my dreams and says she's never going to let me go.

The night before I'm sentenced and shipped out to borstal I dream that I am a big fat African chief sitting on a pile of ivory, with gold coins falling from the sky. Mud huts surround me, but one by one they crumble into dust. As I hold my hand out to catch the gold, it turns into dust too, and when I look down I'm sitting on a pile of snakes. I panic and begin to fall through the pit of snakes into a jungle, and as I fall I hear the sound of screaming women and the pounding of horses hooves, which deafens me. When I try to look at who it is screaming beneath me, more gold and ivory falling from the sky blinds me. I wake up wondering who the hell this chief is who has been following me all my life.

33

"We don't get many of your sort here," says the church minister.

"What do you mean?" I ask.

"One of you Dr Barnardo's kids in borstal. Very rare, that is. What went wrong?"

"There's another one of us in Dover, so that blows your theory."

I sit all hunched up in his cubby hole. Snake has got a grip of me, and since I've been inside, I can't escape her hiss. The minister asks me to look at him; I avoid his eyes and play with a buckle on my Italian handmade shoes.

"So what happened?"

I keep looking at the floor and pretend I can't hear. But Snake lets me know that she definitely can. "None of your fucking business."

"What religion are you?"

"You're joking. What, I've gotta go to church in this shithole?"

"If you want the Lord's help. Yes."

"Don't preach to me about fucking God. Where was he when I fucking needed him?"

"Blasphemous as well. You really are a rotten Dr

Barnardo's kid."

"And you're the devil's incarnation. Now get me out of here."

The dent in his forehead narrows, he shudders a little, and I know I've stung him where it hurts. "It's your choice. If you want to remain a sinner, then do as you please. But I'm here for you every week if you want to change."

He's so fucking nice about it that I calm down a little. "No thanks. But you can put me down as Church of England."

Snake whips me in my stomach so that I almost throw up. I manage to stop myself and say: "No, put me down as agnostic; that's what I am."

"Time's up," booms a screw. She takes hold of her keys and leads me through several doors to my new home, Borstal. Along the way I pass women with love bites daisy-chained around their necks. They vampire my neck by staring at me seductively, and I flinch, not knowing where to put my eyes.

I'm on B house. It has two floors with cells inserted all around the walls. The wing is on the ground floor and you can look all the way up to the first floor. I'm taken upstairs onto the first floor balcony, which has metal railings to try and put us off jumping into the ground floor wing. The screw unlocks a heavy door and ushers me in and I am greeted by two white plastic pisspots, two beds and a shelf. "Make yourself at home," she says, slamming the door shut and locking it behind her. I sit on my new bed and wonder what my new cellmate will look like. I look around the scarce room and notice that she smokes roll-ups, wears crimplene and Clarks shoes, and reads *Linda Lovelace's Diary*. I hope I don't end up like this.

I can hear the judge saying "Six months to two years, and

it's up to you how long you do." I tell myself I could be out in seven months on good behaviour, well before my seventeenth birthday. I had my sixteenth on remand, and I was not going to have another one inside. Snake takes hold of my thoughts. She has different plans for me. She sends me into a drunken doze and I begin to hallucinate. Snake emerges with her whole body coiling on four walls. She looks down at me from the ceiling, shedding her skin into my lap. She curses me with "Judas, traitor, cheat." The words reverberate in my head, and I know that voice, but I can't remember who it belongs to. I look down at the snakeskin, admiring its beauty, wishing it were a pair of shoes. And then the keys jangle in the lock and the door is pulled open by a screw. Snake coils herself back inside my body and I can't move.

In walks a young woman dressed in a long shirt with a belt round it to make it look like a dress. I notice her neck, and she says: "Oh, don't worry about those, toothpaste gets rid of them. And in any case, they won't show up on your skin, so you've got no fear of being put on report."

I sit still and don't say a word. The echoes of Snake's words are bugging me. I desperately want to remember who the voice belongs to.

"You must be Sherry's sister. How come you're black and she's white?"

Her question arrests me and I'm able to reconnect to my voice. "We were in a children's home together."

"Oh, so it's not blood."

"As good as."

She picks her nose and wipes it on the lime-green manky wall. "So what are you? Straight, lezzo or prison bent?"

"What's prison bent?"

"Done bird in the Hole and you dunno what prison bent is? Where was you when I was born?"

I look at her and scan her face. I smile and reply: "In Africa." I'm as surprised by my answer as she is.

"Weirdo or what? Prison bent is when you screw men on the outside, and when you do time here you screw girls. Got it. So what are you?"

I hesitate, look at her mauled neck and say, "I don't know."

"Whaddya mean you dunno? Who do you screw?"

"Nobody."

She sits on her pisspot, looks up at me and says, "Liar, you must be homo."

"Homo I'm not, I'm not in the nude for it," and then I giggle.

"It's not a joking matter. You need to know," and then she splashes into her pot for almost sixty seconds. "There are a few rules you need to learn around here."

"Such as?"

"Look here, Princess, none of us gonna be your wet nurse in here. I know those old biddies in the Hole. They adopt you young 'uns as their babies and by the time you get to borstal you're still green with your nappies on. Spoilt fucking rotten. That's what I say." She pauses and laughs out aloud: "Sherry's sister indeed. Well I never," and then she launches into another lecture.

"For a start you need to know which way you swing." She lets out a big fart, smiles, gets up from the pot, wipes her backside, puts the lid back on before she can catch the smell. "And no shit parcels."

"No what?"

"No shit parcels," and she sprays bouquet of flower deodorant, making the smell ten times worse. "No shitting in newspapers and slinging it out of the window. Always use your pisspot. Got it."

"Sure, sure."

"Never trust a screw. They're all Rottweilers and will savage you in the back. Even if you sit down and drink tea with them, they'll pretend to like you." I twist my face up at the thought of tea.

"Don't worry, luv, the tea is okay here. Not like the Hole. No floating scum in mugs. It's laced with much less bromide. The girls are much hornier here," and she shows off her neck again. "What was I saying?"

"Don't trust a screw."

"Yep, that's right, if they're friendly, all they're doing is snooping for gossip. In other words, don't ever grass. Got it?"

And before I can say something, she's in my face telling me to nick all the new dish cloths or white bootlaces I see lying around. "They're great for burning at night when we're banged up and desperate for a smoke," she says.

"I don't smoke."

"Well, you better learn fast, and make sure you learn how to swing a dolly bag at night when some of us need a light. Are you sure you're Sherry's sister?"

"Yes, why?"

"You're so fucking posh and Miss Prim-and-Proper. You should be white and her black. You better watch your step; there're a few bullies, and you're one of the spring chickens in here, so watch it. So what are you in for?"

"Shoplifting."

"I might have guessed," and she looks at my cashmere suit longingly. "You'll be wearing crimplene in a month."

"Are you sure?"

She laughs: "Trust me. Oh, by the way, my name is Trace and I'm in for GBH. Oh, here we go again, it's the operatic keys; you'll learn to love that tune. It's slop-out time."

The weighty door hurls open and in walks the same screw that brought me to my cell. "Hope you've been telling Pauline all she needs to know to get out of here in seven months," she says with her eyebrows raised. Trace just barges past her with the pisspot in her hand and leaves me standing, not knowing where to go. I wonder how Sherry is doing next door in the other house. The governor made it clear when I arrived that I couldn't live on the same house as her.

I'm initiated at my first meal. Splat, a piece of sausage lands on my forehead from out of space. I look up and most people are grinning. "Welcome. Hope you're as bad as your sister Sherry. My name is Trix." She is built like a bull terrier and most people are petrified of her, including the screws. She flicks another bit of sausage and then everyone joins in, some aiming at the screws that are policing the tea urns nearby. Every piece misses as nobody wants to lose time for assaulting a screw. I head back to my cell after tea, but Trace grabs my arms and says: "You better time your body to go to the loo." So I follow the crowd into the toilets and tiptoe between the bird shit, tampons and hair cemented to the floor. I get to know some other girls while waiting to use the bogs. Some are in for stealing cars, others for burglary and drugs, GBH, and most of us for shoplifting. I settle in quickly, as Sherry has paved the way; she's thrown every bit of abuse she can think of at the screws. She kisses her teeth at any one of them who dares to come within spitting distance of her and leaves a trail of broken furniture behind her. So people are cautious of me and leave me alone.

34

Hawk is the head of my house. She wears goggles that take up most of her face, and dangles right over you when she speaks to you. She's the nicest of the bunch, knows how to laugh, and turns the other way when you're up to no good. The rest of the screws are so uptight that you can hear their arses squeak when they walk. Dare to disagree with any of them and they'll sling you behind the door as quick as thunder and lightning, waiting to be put on report. Loss of all privileges while you're still up on the wing. But nobody gives a toss as the screws are on strike most days, so we spend all our time behind the door, except for work, school, meals and slop out.

I can see that there are roaming Spirits who have evicted some of the inmates from their bodies, while others have someone living on their shoulders. But nobody seems to notice except me. When Trace begins to jump up and down just before we're banged up after tea, I can see her cat pushing her towards the riot bell. She tries hard to pull away, but the cat jerks her hand onto the bell. Screws come running in and she is carried head-first, down to the punishment block. She sees the governor the next morning and arrives back upstairs later in the day, with an extra week tagged onto her sentence.

Sherry and I are allowed to meet every other week once the screw strike is called off. She's managed to complete her borstal in ten months. When her time comes closer for her to leave, she promises me money in the bank, and gold on my wrists. She's already planned a trip while inside, to go and sell American Express and other credit cards in Switzerland. But although my Snake is attracted to her, I know I can't go on. I don't know how to explain that I want to get rid of my Snake, that I want my body back. Because whenever I try to broach the subject, her cats throw her upside down and everything is broken in her sight.

A screw comes charging in and says: "I don't bloody care if you're family; any more fights and your visits will be banned."

I'm silent, and Sherry can feel me pulling away, so we argue over how long we've got left of our fifteen minutes every time we meet, up until the day she leaves.

She keeps her promise. A few weeks after her departure, my whole house is woken up by screams and laughter. She has broken into the grounds with Bog Roll and Needles, who were shipped out on the same bus. "Lower your fucking dolly bags," one of them calls out. Some others and me come to the windows and do as we are told. "Here. Don't say I don't love you," Sherry says. I pull my bag up and find a block of hash, a packet of cigarettes, a fifty-pound note, and some yellow pills.

Trace ambushes me and tussles for my bag. She jumps to the window, and says: "Thanks. So what's it like on the outside?"

"Don't like it," says Bog Roll.

"Yeah, it's much better here," says Needles. "At least you

don't have to worry about money, rent, food and clothes."

"Quick, it's a flashlight," shouts Sherry.

"We love you," they all cry out aloud, and then make a dash back into the dark.

Several doors including mine are flung open. I'm body-searched along with ten others. Trace has stashed the drugs in the pisspot, and the money is shoved up her cunt.

When the screws have done their rounds, and only find a lighter in the next-door neighbour's cell, the lights are switched back out. Half an hour later there is a tap on the pipes: it's the code to say someone wants a light.

"Trace, Pauline, get to your windows," calls Stammer. "There's no pretending you're asleep tonight. Word is out, you've got candy."

I poke my head through the window and a navy dolly bag hanging from a long torn piece of green counterpane is already swinging its way to our window. There is a white bootlace smouldering away from its bottom, being sent to give us a light. Stammer, who lives four windows along and on the floor above says, "Don't say I never think of you," and lets out a chuckle while swinging the dolly bag next door to Jade. "And that gift from Sherry can't possibly be for you, Pauline, you're so squeaky clean," she adds.

Trace muscles in at the window and says, "I'm taking care of this package," and a slanging match begins. But it stops almost as soon as it starts, as nobody will come to their window in between Jade's cell and ours. So Jade has to try and swing across the barren window to Olivia, who is directly above us. After the fourth attempt she makes it and the bag is lowered down. Trace takes a light from the lace and rations the goodies out. Olivia snatches it back up, empties out her treats and swings it back to the impatient hungry girls. Trace orders me to open my mouth. She shoves a piece of hash and a pill in my gob and says: "Close your eyes and think of heaven."

I gulp it down and hold my breath, waiting for something to happen. But nothing does so I do what I am told and close my eyes. I'm woken up by the same hissing voice accusing me of being a Judas, a traitor and a cheat. I sit up and look around the room, thinking I should recognise the person cursing me, but all I can see is Snake's shadow writhing on the ceiling. Trace is fast asleep so I can't accuse her, so I go back asleep again and find myself falling through the jungle, with ivory, gold and snakeskin pelting at my feet. Before I reach the bottom I am disturbed by Trace trying to wake me up. "Quick, get up, otherwise the screws will suspect something."

I pull myself together as I think about my dream. I know it so well now that it bugs me every time.

Trace leaves borstal a week later. She won three of her months back for good behaviour. As soon as she has gone, Florence is moved in. She hides behind a shaggy mane of chestnut hair, shuffles along the floor in slippers from the Co-op and mutters only when you speak to her. Her cat has sucked all her energy and makes Florence dozy most of the time. She's inside for stealing a toothbrush and is picked on by everybody for being a docile moron. Everyone stops bullying her when she moves in with me, under the proviso she stops throwing shit parcels out of the window. So it's a happy compromise.

"Pauline, let's speak," calls out Olivia after we're banged up for the night. "It's time we put Florence to work."

"Oh, leave it out, what's she done to you?"

"No, no, it's not like that, I've got a plan."

"I'm all ears for this one. The last plans you had lost me one month. Remember?"

"Which one was that?"

"Fire extinguishers ring a bell? Barricading ourselves in the toilets of the cardboard factory, and spraying the screws when they came to get us."

"Gotta admit it was a laugh."

"An expensive one at that."

"All right, you've made your point. But I mean business this time. Florence works in the laundry. Well, I reckon if we get her to nick the counterpanes, I could get some girls to make up boxers in the sewing factory, while they're making up shorts for the male prisons. Look, I've got a pattern."

Stammer comes to the window and says: "Yeah, that's a great idea, and while you lot are keeping me awake, pass me a light."

"Shit," Olivia squeals.

"Well, what do you expect? There's no privacy out of these windows. Now swing me a flipping light."

Olivia takes her smouldering lace which is hanging off her dolly bag from her window and manages to swing across two windows without waking anybody else up.

Stammer is delighted with her late night smoke, and whispers loudly: "So it's a deal, green and blue boxers, they'll look pretty stylish in here."

"Exactly, we can trade them," replies Olivia.

With our heads hanging out of the window, the three of us swear ourselves to secrecy about our plan while everyone is supposed to be asleep.

In a week I'm falling asleep to the scent of Old Holborn leaking out of my pillowcase. I have dreams of Uncle Boris in Cross Cottage, of my two dogs, Duke and Duchess, and Annabel flies into my dreams and tells me I must pray to

God for his forgiveness. It's the closest I've felt to Annabel in a long while and I wonder if the scent will seduce her back. But instead of Annabel coming to my rescue I'm inundated with orders from the two other houses for shorts. It costs two bars of soap and a bottle of shampoo or a packet of old Holborn and papers for a pair of boxers. I get so much tobacco that even Florence can't smoke it all, so I stuff it under my mattress and hope that Annabel will at least enter my dreams again.

Instead my door lumbers open at 6am. Hawk enters, reading the riot act on the infamous white sheet, stating my charges: "Pauline Charles, you are under house arrest for the following charges. Inciting trouble on the house. One of the ringleaders of the Boxer racket. Being in possession of toiletries and tobacco through illicit means." And then they pounce, eight screws on my arms and legs, dragging me head-first off the wing, through a corridor swamped with every screw they could rustle up that morning.

I'm high by 6.15am, with the biggest ever endorphin rush I can imagine. Stammer and Olivia swiftly follow, each of us landing down in the punishment block in style.

"Liveaway" we call it. Solitary confinement in a dingy dank cell. A foam mattress hides all the garbage from the past residents. Its stench becomes a pungent aroma by day two, and I can't tell if it is me who needs a scrub or the cell. Ziggy has scrawled her name with her faeces on the wall, and Chaz has scratched her signature with an illegal object. I entertain myself by trying to do the splits in a strip dress, which only allows my legs five inches of freedom or a slow jog on the spot. It's made out of a toughened starched nylon that I can't tear, in the hope of preventing my death through hanging. My heart sinks as I stare at the bleak four walls. I am down the block again, with KN6071 chalked on to my cell door. I can hardly hear my mates Stammer or Olivia when they call to see if I am still alive. If I'm lucky I get to bang on their doors when I'm let out of my cell for a five-minute sniff in the quad. But most days the screws forget us, and we're left to languish in the cell. The governor adds two months onto our borstal sentences and places all of us on Her Majesty's Pleasure. She will decide in her own time when she sees fit for all of us to go back onto the house.

Some days I watch the day turn from bright light to dusk to pitch through the barbed wired window. If the sun is shining in the right direction it makes beautiful mosaics on my walls and I can pretend I am tripping on Lady Esquire. Some nights are spent screaming at the mystery person tapping on the pipes and other days are spent catching up on sleep. The minister comes to visit me and preaches at me through the hatch. "I can see you're possessed," he says one day, and my body begins to tremble violently. I look at him and am half-relieved that somebody has finally seen my Snake.

The other part of me withdraws and Snake takes over my body completely, throwing myself at the door. "Go get a life," I bawl. The next morning, he pushes a Bible in and tells me to repent. I take hold of it and tear it to shreds to use as toilet paper as it's rationed most days.

I open my pot to crap and the page with Deuteronomy 6 damp but unsmeared, is staring me in the face. The stench makes me comatose and I can't move. I just gawk at the page: "Honour thy father and thy mother, as the Lord thy God have commanded thee."

I glance down the page and read: "Thou shalt not kill, neither shalt thou steal." I vomit, puking all over my pisspot. With the rest of the shredded Bible, I mop up the mess and throw up all over again, collapsing onto the floor into a hazy stupor.

I am instantly falling through the jungle and, as I fall, I am looking at myself. I'm the proud chief of a Yoruba village, sitting on a pile of ivory, surrounded by gold. I hear my father, mother, my sisters, brothers, and friends all screaming for help. The sound of horses' hooves make me look up and I can hear somebody shouting Judas, traitor, cheat. As I turn to see who it is, they disappear and my life unwinds before my eyes.

I witness my Spirit passing through several rebirths. I'm a peasant wandering nomadically in the hills. I'm a hunter and a food gatherer. There is a landslide and I am displaced in foreign lands. I'm still of peasant stock next time I'm reborn, but the land is so harsh that my whole family dies of hunger. On my deathbed I make a pact with myself that nobody in my family will ever die of poverty again. Next time round I'm so desperate not to be reborn as a peasant, I manage to choose a respectable family to inhabit, and each time I die, my rebirth is more prosperous until I become a chief.

The first time I become chief, I drown. The second time I'm born into chiefdom I am successful. However, not content with being the chief of a village and with all my riches, my Spirit craves even more. I see my chance of ensuring everlasting wealth. I exchange my parents, siblings and many of the village men and women to slave owners for ivory and gold. "Payback," the familiar voice screams. I wake up thinking someone has just called my name. I look around at the mess in my cell, and the only thing I can remember from my dream is the word "payback".

35

I meet Cutes through the hatch. "You look as if you've just seen a ghost," she teases.

Embarrassed with the state of my cell, I flippantly reply: "Yes, you."

I shudder and I find myself saying sorry under my breath. She ignores my remark and stands on the other side, pushing my meal plate into my hands. "You must be Cutes everyone has been gossiping about?" I ask. She smiles shyly, loiters for a few seconds and then slams my hatch flap shut. News had come down to the block that there was a really cute new black screw working on my house.

I let the sound of Cutes's footsteps and keys around her hips make sweet music to my ears. I empty my liver, mashed potatoes and peas on top of this morning's excrement and vomit, and wish for her to come and take me out for my whiff of fresh air. However, it's my plastic crockery she wants when she returns to my hatch an hour later. Her warm smile takes me off balance and I can feel my eyes welling up. I feel as if I'm losing the plot, and all I want to do is scream aloud: "Sorry; I'm sorry, please forgive me." But she's gone before I can let my first scream out.

The next time I see Cutes it's a week later at 10.30am

with the governor. She opens the door and the governor, flanked by three of her staff, puts one foot in my cell and offers me a taste of freedom. It's been a month since all three of us have been incarcerated and now I can go upstairs to the land of the living and be banged up in my room for another two more weeks, with my name – Pauline Charles – chalked outside. Olivia went up last week, and I leave Stammer behind. It's obvious they need my cell for someone else.

Cutes opens my hatch and pushes some Oxfam clothes through.

Five minutes later she's calling to me, asking if I'm ready and dressed to go up. I'm lulled by her husky soft voice and feel overwhelmed with remorse. Snake even approves as she doesn't create when Cutes opens my door and guides me back up to my cell. Once I'm home I dress up in my Cecil Gee cardigan, silk shirt and Farrah trousers, and dance around my cell in a pair of Bally shoes. I hang out of my window and watch the traffic pass underneath. I make friends with Cutes, who passes at 4pm every day to collect the workers from the factory. I entertain myself by counting the shit parcels that have been thrown out and get into frivolous banter with Cutes.

"Hey, sugar," I hackney to death out of the window. But Cutes always turns and smiles.

"Not you, the other lump."

"Don't you think that's a bit old hat?"

"No," and we laugh and become friends through one-liners and quick replies. She gives me soundbites about her husband, children and family life. And for the first time I begin to feel homesick and think about all my friends.

I can feel Snake pining in my heart. Snake has been number one since Annabel hasn't been around. And she hasn't left much room for anyone else. Whenever Cutes is about my hiss seems to fade and all I can hear is the thrashing of my heart. My two weeks fly by and I am back out on the wing with all my rights and privileges. Cutes and I have become close after two weeks of speaking daily from the window, and some screws ask if I'm bribing her because they've never seen me so calm, gentle and generous with a prison officer before.

I'm banged up again in my cell two days after being let out. This time I get to do "liveaway" behind the door in my own cell. I threw a shoe at Olivia for getting on my case, about being friends with a screw. Cutes calls up to my window: "In trouble again, Pauline? I hear you've got another week behind the door."

I drag myself to the window and ask her: "What's it to do with you?"

"I care about you, Pauline. Don't you care about yourself?"

"Nope!"

"Well, you should."

"Go fuck yourself."

"Have it your way, Pauline, but when you're older you'll regret it."

I kiss my teeth, and put myself to bed. I know Cutes wants me to think about my life. But living has felt like I've been hurtling down a never-ending slide since I went to live with Wunmi, and I'm too scared to stop skidding down the slide. Whenever I try to stop, my head feels as if it's going to burst, and Snake wraps herself around my neck, causing me to have palpitations. I'm too scared to stop, but I keep on being friends with Cutes as she is the only thing which makes me feel good.

Some of my mates continue to tease me for lapping up to a screw, but I don't care as Cutes feels like a mum I've never had. Snake is peaceful, and I feel like I've met someone who really cares although I'm not sure I want to start caring if it means I have to begin taking responsibility for my actions. Whenever Cutes tries to talk sense to me I tell her: "It's the system's fault that I'm inside. Not mine. And I want them to pay."

"You're only hurting yourself, Pauline. Nobody else."

"Who the hell are you to tell me what I'm doing?"

I look down at her red-black face and hope she can see that I'm sorry.

There has been a high turnover of inmates since I've been behind the door. Florence has been moved on to another house and at least five people have left. There is a group of four new young women who seem to be running the roost.

They beat up women behind the door, tax inmates for their baccy and toiletries and create havoc at work. Olivia and Stammer join the gang and try to persuade me, but I've made a pact with Cutes that I'm going to try and keep out of trouble.

It's my first Saturday on the wing in two months and everyone is hanging out trying to have some fun. I walk into the recreation room and I almost lose my balance. Snake is shrieking like mad and thrashing away in my stomach. I look across the room and see the gang have one of the new timid inmates pinned to the floor. One of them has hold of a broomstick and is ramming it between her legs. Stammer has her hands cupped over her mouth while the others take turns using deodorant bottles too. "Wanna go?" one of the gang says, and then laughs. I can't move. Wunmi and several women who look like me flash before my eyes. Snake takes a hold of me, ripping my guts inside out.

Snake screams out loud again in my head: "Judas, traitor,

cheat!" She irritates me as I can't work out who that voice belongs to. I take a look at the young woman, who is left sobbing on the floor. For a second she looks like Wunmi and I run like mad out of the room into my cell. Snake is in my head, bellowing, "Payback, you fool, payback!"

I crash and wake up to the sound of mugs banging on the window ledges. My house is singing out to Sandy, who lives in the house next door to us. "We love you, Sandy, oh yes we do, we love you, Sandy, and that is true, we love you, Sandy, we do. Oh, Sandy, we love you." And one by one she sings as loud as she can to all her best mates on our house that she loves them. She promises never to come back, but in a month she arrives in my cell, on her third borstal.

I can't believe today has actually arrived. I'm leaving tomorrow. I've lost so much time that I've forgotten that one day I would have to say goodbye. I end up doing twelve months including my time in the Hole. I'm out two months before my seventeenth birthday. Cutes comes to congratulate me on my last night, and says, "See, I told you, you could do it." She whispers her telephone number in my ear. Bangs me up one last time. Sandy, my new cellmate, wants to know what the secret is about. I wink and before she can ask me any more questions, we are both assaulted by the loud banging of mugs on the ledges.

"Everyone to the windows," Olivia shouts. And all three houses come to their windows with their plastic mugs. "One, two, three," she screams and they all begin to sing me out.

"Good luck, good health, God bless you," and the plastic mugs are banged against the brick walls. "And guide you on your way." Bang bang. "There's a ship a leaving borstal today." Bang bang. "It's taking poor Pauline away. There stand her mates with their arms open wide, singing Pauline we love you, we do. We'll always be faithful and true, so give us a hug, instead of the bug, and we'll be missing you."

Bang crash whollop, go the mugs on the outside walls. I sing to my mates one by one and tell them I love them I do.

I swing my last dolly bag and sit on my pisspot for the last time. Delirious from my farewell party I fall asleep on top of my bed, fully clothed.

"That's who it is," I call out in my sleep. And my cellmate throws a pillow and says: "Shut the fuck up." I undress myself and quietly put myself to bed. But Snake won't let me sleep so I just lie under my covers. I close my eyes and try to imagine sheep jumping over a stile, but before I get to one, I'm back in my dream.

Snake takes a hold of my body again and throws me through the bed. I lose my breath. Paralysed by what I see while looking down on the river Oshun, my heart misses every drumbeat. I can see my Spirit being seduced again by the thought of being a love child. My heart begins to pound as I realise I chose my wife from a past life to be my mother in this life and bring me back into the world. The voice in my head is Wunmi. It's my wife too. She never forgave me for selling our people, and the rapes of all the village women. She poisoned me in my sleep. Since then I've been lingering for hundreds of years not healthy enough to reincarnate. And finally almost seventeen years ago, I managed to be reborn. Snake's cry becomes so loud that it penetrates my whole body like the hiss of the venom which belonged to the snake that took me to my last grave.

Just as I begin to fall through the jungle again I wake upright in my bed, soaked from head to toe, screaming out loud: "Payback!" My cell is flanked with screws, with a doctor beside my bed. He takes hold of my arm and injects it with a dose of something to calm my nerves. "But my dream," I cry.

"It's all right," the doctor says. "It happens to a lot of you young women on your last night. This will make you sleep and you won't even know that I came to say goodbye to you on your last night." The screws lead him out and Sandy demands to know: "Who the hell is fucking Snake?"

The dose is so strong that I'm dead to the world in a flash. And the next moment Sandy is telling me to get up. I sit up and look at my sports bag filled to the brim with all my clothes. "My dream," I say to Sandy.

"Oh not again. I had that all last night."

"Last night?"

"And as for bloody payback! Take this, you rat bag, as I can't get you back tonight." And she jumps up and down beside my bed repeating "Snake, Snake, Snake" until she drives me bonkers. I put my hands to my ears and muffle Sandy's chant. She stops and says: "Come on, you're supposed to be happy; it's your last fucking day."

"My dream," I plead again.

And she walks out of the room, saying: "I'll see you at breakfast."

I sit wedged on my bed trying really hard to remember what I just dreamt. But I can't, it's gone. My mates come rushing in like vultures, looking to raid my toiletries and anything else they can lay their hands on.

"Have the lot," and I point to my Slazenger sports bag that has followed me around the streets. One of the women grabs it, scavenges through the lot, chucking out my silk shirts, Farrahs, cashmeres, Jaegar and Aquascutum suits and Burberry to the floor. "Take the lot, I don't want it." They leave me my knickers, bras and my socks, and rush off leaving me starkers, still sitting in bed while I try to recall my dream. I still can't remember a thing, but I know I have to make my peace with Snake. She is still borrowing my body and seething away in the background. I get dressed in a crimplene skirt and a polyester crew neck jumper that Trace, my first cellmate, gave to me before she left.

I remember the day she walked out free, teasing me that one day it will be my turn and I'll be dressed up to the nines just like her. And she's right. I can't believe my day of freedom has finally come around too.

After breakfast I am greeted by smiling screws all dressed in blue, lined up to bid me farewell. I see them as human beings for the first time, and try to see if I can remember any of their proper names. But I can't so I smile sweetly and swear on oath that I will never come back again. Some of them just smile back as if they have heard it all before. Hawk makes a point of patting me on my back and says: "There's some hope with you. You're still a juvenile, you've got a chance, grab it if you can."

Hawk takes me to the doors of freedom. I say my final goodbye, step into the van. I sit in the back all on my own. I look through the window, and last night's dream begins to haunt me again. I am face to face with Snake. Besieged with remorse, I uncontrollably break down. "I'm sorry," I whisper to myself. Snake calms down in my body and I feel light, like a feather just plucked from a bird. Through bleary eyes I stare at the trees along the driveway that I planted while working on the farm and know I will never see them come of age. Minutes later I board a train. I open a window and bask my face in the sunlight. I feel parched. Thirsting for life like never before, I quench my first new breath of fresh air. A butterfly lands on my forehead. I smile.

"Friends forever," I whisper. I pick my plastic carrier bag off the seat. It has everything in the world I own. I empty out onto the railway tracks my gold necklaces, bracelets, rings, and the few items of clothes I adore. Snake feels dormant in my body. My heart beats fast as I watch the green pastures whiz by.

Kin: New Fiction by Black and Asian Women

Edited by Karen McCarthy

'*Kin* is a sharp, contemporary collection of short stories from the next generation of black and Asian women writers, and as such it is a platform for a new literature unique to the UK' Karen McCarthy

The presence of black and Asian people in the UK has altered the nation in so many ways that our culture is now one of fusion. Against this backdrop, *Kin* brings together some of the sharpest new literary talent, from the poetic intensity of Francesca Beard and the assured prose of Donna Daley-Clarke, to the electric energy of Gemma Weekes, riding the crest of the wave on her 'Gucci broomstick'. The stories in *Kin* are populated by a fascinating cast of characters, sometimes bizarre, always intriguing. This collection brings together the finest of the new voices.

Contributors are: Jamika Ajalon, Francesca Beard, Donna Daley-Clarke, Krishna Dutta, Diana Evans, Barbara Graham, Amanthi Harris, Heather Imani, Sharon Jennings, Kalbinder Kaur, Shiromi Pinto, Ranbir Sahota, Nicola Sinclair, Saradha Soobrayen, Gemma Weekes.

'Fifteen stories by black and Asian women, and every single one of them a bona fide diamond... each of these narratives is vivid and moving. Perfect of themselves, all are unusual encapsulations of modern life, and most tempered by historical forces that differ from the white British experience... The rhythm of this anthology is superb, with highs and lows, fantasy and reality, horrors and hardships, all balanced in generous measure' *Venue*

We Need to Talk About Kevin

Lionel Shriver

Two years ago, Eva Khatchadourian's son, Kevin, murdered seven of his fellow high-school students, a cafeteria worker, and a popular algebra teacher. Because he was only fifteen at the time of the killings, he received a lenient sentence and is now in a prison for young offenders in upstate New York. Telling the story of Kevin's upbringing, Eva addresses herself to her estranged husband through a series of letters. Fearing that her own shortcomings may have shaped what her son has become, she confesses to a deep, long-standing ambivalence about motherhood in general and Kevin in particular. How much is her fault?

Lionel Shriver tells a compelling, absorbing, and resonant story while framing these horrifying tableaux of teenage carnage as metaphors for the larger tragedy – the tragedy of a country where everything works, nobody starves, and anything can be bought but a sense of purpose.

'A book about the dangerous distance that exists between what we feel and what we are prepared to admit when it comes to family life… a book about what we need to talk about but can't'
Rachel Cusk, *Guardian*

'As a mother of two, reading Lionel Shriver's novel *We Need to Talk About Kevin* was a comfort and a revelation. I'm not the only one who agonised over what the impact of having a child would be, felt invaded by pregnancy and was terrified at the awesome responsibility of becoming a mother and being held responsible for whatever adult I turn out. It's a profoundly important novel with universal appeal. It's beautifully written and a sometimes shocking, but always gripping read.' Jenni Murray, BBC *Woman's Hour*

Finding Fish

Antwone Fisher

Antwone Fisher was raised in institutions in Ohio from the moment of his birth in prison to a single mother. For many years he lived with the Picketts, a cruel and uncaring foster family who abused him physically and mentally. Desperate for a better life, Antwone Fisher enlisted in the US Navy where he found friendship and emotional support. *Finding Fish* shows how, out of this unlikely mix of deprivation and hope, an artist was born – first as the child who painted the feelings his words dared not speak, then as a poet and storyteller who would eventually become one of Hollywood's most sought-after screenwriters.

A *New York Times* bestseller, *Finding Fish* is an incredible tale of personal triumph in the face of the bleakest adversity. It reaffirms the reader's faith in the power of human survival.

'*Finding Fish* reads like a great work of fiction, moving me alternately to tears and laughter, sorrow and joy, and making me forget at times that the story is astonishingly true' Denzel Washington

'This stunning autobiography rises above the success fables from survivors of America's inner cities' *Publisher's Weekly*

'*The Color Purple*, but true male and set in the 1960s!... Fisher's searing, luminous portrait transcends the familiar, as does his retroactive tenderness toward the boy no one else loved' *Time*

'His intense and impassioned style inspires and imbues from start to finish. This is a story that juxtaposes laughter and profound sadness, evokes ambivalence and leaves a lasting impression on the human soul... This offering is a testament to an indomitable spirit that refuses to be broken – even in the face of extreme adversity' *Pride Magazine*

Heredity

Jenny Davidson

Smart, blonde, and self-destructive, Elizabeth Mann thinks that leaving New York for a London travel-writing job will solve all her problems. She couldn't be more wrong: in a museum of medical curiosities at the Royal College of Surgeons, her daydreams over the skeleton of Jonathan Wild – a notorious eighteenth-century bounty-hunter – are interrupted by an encounter with Gideon Streetcar, an attractive gynaecologist with asthma and a low sperm count.

As Elizabeth fast assumes the humiliating, exhilarating role of Gideon's secret mistress, her obsession with Jonathan Wild grows. At an auction she happens upon the diary of Wild's own mistress, who was also named Elizabeth Mann. Further tantalized by this coincidence, Elizabeth decides that with Gideon's help, she will give birth to the bounty-hunter's clone. An impressive debut, *Heredity* is a virtuoso tale about the world of fertility and genetic cloning.

'A wild cocktail of perverse historical romance, criminal cloning, adulterous sex, and medical shenanigans – Georgette Heyer meets Daniel Defoe and the Marquis de Sade' Michèle Roberts

'The book is laced with veins of fascinating minutiae about grave robbing by early anatomists, the mechanics of vitro fertilization, even the pathology of syphilis' *New York Times Book Review*

'Drawing its author comparisons to writers from A.S. Byatt to Susanna Kaysen, Davidson's dark debut, *Heredity*, is the stuff of biology, love, and self-destruction – you know, like all the good books' *Seattle Stranger*

'*Heredity* is a marvelously entertaining work of intellectual and biological obsession – bawdy, audacious, and very funny' David Liss, author of *The Coffee Trader* and *A Conspiracy of Paper*